Montserrat

Montserrat

a novel

FRANKLIN LAFAYETTE KING

*t*P
Texture Press
2015

Copyright © 2015 Franklin Lafayette King

Published in the United States by
Texture Press
1108 Westbrooke Terrace
Norman, OK 73072

For ordering information,
visit the Texture Press website at
www.texturepress.org

Cover concept and painting:
Franklin Lafayette King

Book design: Arlene Ang

ISBN-13: 978-0-692-57742-4
ISBN-10: 0-692-57742-4

Also by Franklin Lafayette King

Novels

The Dark Side of Man
The Story of James and Other Writings
The Woman in the Window
The Seven Woods of Coole
In the Shadow of Leaves
Lost Graves

Poetry

Sunflowers and Zinnias
Hauntings of a Summer Moon
The Poet Who Writes upon Water

Montserrat

The Soufriere Hills volcano spews smoke, ash and debris upon the Caribbean island of Montserrat. The mountain exhales its breath into the warm tropical air. Plymouth, the capital of the island, lies buried in the pyroclastic flow.

Montserrat is known by two names that define its personality: Pompeii and the Emerald Island of the Caribbean. Like the nature of man, it too is bipolar. With a change in mood, Montserrat will be destroyed again either by hurricane or violent eruption only to be reborn under the tropical sun.

Dedicated to Pamela
whose advice I have taken

Montserrat

The warm sea surrounds you.
Sky and sea blend in a tourist's drink.

Island bred upon the bed of the sea.
Two personalities yet birthed as one.

Julie mango and lemon trees
A jigger of rum, please, pour for me.

Africa and Ireland mixed
with whiskey and tropic sun.

Bones of Plymouth, village and farm.
Nightmares of ash and tropic storm

I have followed the rivers of the sea
from Fomhoire to Stinky Toe.

While you are up,
a bowl of goat's head stew for two.

Like the woman of the night, between two lovers she resides,
violent or docile, take your pick.

Do you now lie upon the sands of Carr's or Little Bay?
The breath of the sea, red hair and sunburned skin.

Or are you there beneath Soufrière Hills
when the lights of Antigua are seen across the night black sea?

Turmoil of nature and man intertwined
forever evolving never complete.

Table of Contents

Chapter 1
TOWER OF FOMHOIRE

Edmond Bryant was a tenured professor for five years at Fullerton University, a small private liberal arts institution. After a day of meetings, he returned home and checked the mail in the hallway. He sorted the letters between his fingers placing the bills between his index finger and thumb. When he came to a manila envelope with a return address that he recognized, he tore it open, his heart beating loudly.

"April, I can't believe it!" he shouted to his wife of five years. "All the hard work has finally paid off. I have been invited to present to a learned society in Ireland. Not only present, I am the keynote speaker."

"No kidding! Why are you standing by the door and not hugging me?" April ran down the staircase of their small home and leaped into his arms. "A trip to the country I have always wanted to visit. I never thought we would see it together."

After hugging each another, April looked at him seriously. "Will they pay per diem?" They both had sacrificed to save money for their first home and she knew that Edmond's salary was not adequate for such a trip. It was not unusual for academic conferences to pay little or nothing for traveling expenses.

"Even better, they are paying for my flight. Of course, you're coming with me, but the stipend will pay for half of the trip. Tonight let's go to Romano's and celebrate. In fact, we may even have the house wine," he said with a smile.

They both knew the importance of such a presentation to his career. He very much needed the recognition of his peers. Such an honor would help ensure his promotion from assistant to associate professor. A pay raise no matter how small was very much needed if they ever hoped to move out of their small house and start a family. Everything in Boston cost so much more than they had anticipated. They felt honored to live and work in a city they could not afford.

While April's family was very well off financially, his was not. Even though April was to inherit a considerable estate on the death of her mother, she was reluctant to ask for money since it would have offended Edmond's pride. He often said, "It is better to do without than to beg."

They had both become proficient in simplifying their approach towards life. They purchased furniture that was stylish but uncomfortable. The few antiques they bought came from the furnishings of former industrial site offices that had closed down. When traveling, they were used to carrying only the minimum of clothes. Their only means of transportation, his 1969 VW Bug, was purchased while Edmond attended undergraduate school. He knew that if he wanted to pursue an academic career, there would never be enough money to live lavishly. They learned to pride themselves on their minimalist lifestyle.

The next few days were spent planning and preparing for his presentation. He knew how critical an academic audience could be. The least mistake would invite unwanted questions and smirks of disapproval. Since the speech was to be read, he was very fortunate that April was an excellent and critical proofreader. She did not miss even the slightest of details. She was so precise that Edmond often felt a sting from her comments.

Even though April had graduated from a very prestigious university with a doctorate in English, she had been unable to obtain work in the States. There were few demands for such a highly specialized field as Irish Studies. Due to her scholarly interest in Irish poets and authors, she had always longed to visit Ireland.

After packing and sending their two French bulldogs to live with her mother, they boarded Aer Lingus in New York for a direct flight to Ireland. Even though the flight was overnight, neither of them could sleep. Edmond kept the reading light on above him as he studied his notes, only briefly glancing at the progress of the flight on the seatback screen. April spent her time translating English to Irish so she could practice the traditional language. Just as they were both falling asleep, the rising sun illuminated the cockpit of the aircraft. She looked out the window but saw only a gray cover of clouds far below. As the minutes passed, the intensity of the light increased.

When the plane entered the skies above Ireland, it was beautiful to see the varying green colors of the fields. Down below she could see the stone walls that marked the farmers' fields. She was amazed at how straight they were. How perfect a boundary of stone can be when placed by a farmer's hands.

The sights far exceeded April's expectations. Soon the clouds closed in below the plane. After they touched down, rain beat against the surface of the aircraft. The man seated next to April turned to her and said, "Welcome to Ireland. A good tan is hard to come by here."

With pride, she replied, "My husband will be presenting at Trinity. He is the keynote speaker at an international conference." She was immediately embarrassed about blurting out something that would mean so little to anyone else.

Without responding, the stranger rose to dislodge his carry-on from the luggage rack above them. Edmond smiled at the stranger's efforts as he confided to April, "That is a suitcase and not a carry-on. When we boarded, I saw one fellow carrying a guitar case. No wonder we had trouble finding space for our carry-ons."

April sensed that Edmond was tense from lack of sleep. She knew too well the pressure he was under. It wasn't easy to please an academic audience whose favorite sport was verbally attacking the speaker.

Where they planned on staying was very nice and convenient. Brooks Hotel was exceptional in catering to the business class of travelers. The excellent staff would help to make their brief stay a true pleasure. April could sense, however, that Edmond was having a difficult time not worrying.

That evening after a hot bath, she rubbed his shoulders. Their only view was that of a nearby stone wall. "Edmond try to relax," she said gently. "They will love your speech. You are always popular with audiences. It may not hurt to take a Valium before you speak." She kissed his back, slowly, deliberately. "Do you want to make love?"

Edmond turned towards her. "I love you. You know that. I am so nervous and tired that I cannot say yes."

"That is okay. The night is long," she whispered.

He wrapped an arm around her. Soon they fell into a tender sleep, undisturbed yet holding one another.

It turned out that the presentation in Dublin went very well. Afterwards Edmond turned to April. "I didn't mention it, but I have taken two weeks of annual leave in addition to travel time. It is a gift I wanted to give you. I know how much you want to see the sites that so influenced the authors and poets that you love. Can you imagine having the time to walk where James Joyce did, to see Lady Gregory's Coole Park and all the other sites you have only read about? Since we are already in Ireland, I thought we'd make the most of it."

"That is truly wonderful. I know why I married you. You are always so thoughtful. I have always wanted to take the James Joyce audio-guided tour of the city. While waiting for you, I learned that headsets and walking instructions are available in the lobby."

Edmond smiled. "Just to be daring, I have searched the Internet for properties we can look at. You know how I love history. Period properties fascinate me."

"What kind of properties are you talking about?" she asked in a teasing manner.

"I know how much you love romance novels, so I have

been exploring castles that are for sale. Can you believe it? There is one within our price range." He paused. "That is, with some creative financing. It's more fun to look at something when you think you might be able to afford it."

"I am sure it is a fixer-upper." She laughed. "You know how to make a vacation both fun and adventurous. I don't suppose it will hurt to look at it. Have you gotten permission from the agent for us to visit it?"

"Yes, I did. The agent is really friendly. Back in the States, she sent a release form for me to review and sign. Something to the effect that we will not sue her if we get injured exploring the castle. At the low asking price, I can only assume it is in ruins."

"You mean we can go through the castle without anyone accompanying us?"

"Yes, that is what she said. After all, it is made of hand-hewn stone. Not much that a potential buyer can do to damage it and certainly no one will steal a hundred-pound block."

"I can't imagine that happening in the States. You know, letting someone tour a house without a realtor present."

"I am not certain you can call a castle a house," Edmond said, smiling. "I promise you that after we tour the castle, we will return to Dublin and take the James Joyce tour of the city. I promise."

"Where is the castle located?" asked April.

"In the south of Ireland where the weather is much nicer. It also includes some riverfront property. It is in a remote area, so finding a driver that knows the area is critical. Incredibly, our travel agent found a retired detective. Just the perfect person to locate lost property." He paused. "I just wish I brought my fly fishing equipment with me."

"I am glad you didn't. Had you brought it, I would not have seen you for the remainder of the trip," she said with a broad smile

Through their stateside travel agent, Edmond had arranged for a driver to take them to the remote castle located on the River Lee near the town of Macroom in County Cork. The driver, Richard Blake, was tall and thin. His demeanor was one of unwavering seriousness. It was apparent from his mannerisms that he did not like the idea of taking American tourists to see historical sites. He made it clear from their meeting that theirs was the first and only tour he would conduct. After that, he planned to remain truly retired.

Even though the Mercedes limo had a GPS, the address could not be programmed into the device. Upon arriving at a small village that bordered on the river, the driver stopped to ask the local constable for specific directions to the castle.

Upon returning to the vehicle, Richard glanced towards Edmond and April. "This is a very remote spot that you have selected. Fortunately for us, one of the constables and I used to work together several years ago in Oughterard. Without his help, we would never be able to locate it."

As they drove along the narrow road, they crossed a stone bridge under which the River Lee, though shallow at this point, flowed rapidly towards the city of Cork. The river's water appeared to be both cold and clear. Beneath its surface, smooth rocks covering the riverbed were visible.

Soon the driver cut off the well-maintained road. As the

car hit large rocks and potholes, it bounced its passengers violently. Suddenly a crumbling gate lodge loomed before them. Engraved in the lichen-covered stone arch was the name CASTLE FOMHOIRE.

The driver slowed down, then stopped. "Are you sure you want to visit this tower castle?" he asked. "With a name like Fomhoire, I would be leery to even consider exploring it much less purchasing it. Did the agent tell you anything about it?"

Edmond replied, "She mentioned it was a tower castle consisting of five levels. In fact, it was one of the few to be built in Ireland for a native Irishman. As you know, most of the tower castles were built for Anglo-Saxons."

"Well, that may explain, at least in part, the name. Irishmen are always seeking supernatural explanations for all events that transpire. It is in our blood to seek heaven only to find hell." Richard paused, then continued, "It translates, if I remember correctly, 'from the sea.' According to our legends, Fomhoire is the home of the gods of cold, night and death."

April laughed. "If I had known that, I think I would have stayed in our hotel in Dublin. At least I should have taken a sweater. I think the cold comes from the river. For me I prefer the Brooks."

Edmond smiled. "Now April, this is our chance for adventure. You don't want our lives to be too boring now, do you?"

She laughed. "A little boredom does not hurt."

As they drove past a small submerged woodland, the castle appeared before them. Dark and neglected, a small tree grew from the tall stone wall. Green moss clung to the lower portion of the castle. Small slits served as the source of light for the lower floors while larger arched windowless portals provided the only daylight to the higher floors. The roof of slate appeared to be newer than the rest of the castle, yet it too was darkened by the almost black lichen that clung to its steep pitch.

"Why is it so wet here?" asked Edmond.

The driver replied, "This is part of the Gearagh, the submerged woodland that grows along the River Lee. Don't worry, the water that runs through it is pure enough to drink."

"You seem to know a lot about this area," said April with a questioning look.

"My grandmother lived downstream from Macroom. We often visited her while we were growing up."

"I am surprised you never heard of Castle Fomhoire."

"Never had a need to," the driver replied.

As they drove closer to the castle, they could hear the savage barking of dogs.

"Why are so many dogs barking? I don't see any," said April.

Across a small unkempt road from the castle was a large stone house. Stone and metal sheds extended from the back of the dwelling. A man stood in the front yard, observing their approach.

"Hello there," said the driver.

"I don't see many people out here. I suppose that you are wanting to buy the castle?" asked the barrel-chested keeper of animals.

"Not me, the two in the back are wanting to look at it. This kind of place doesn't interest me. We heard a lot of barking a moment ago, what kinds of dogs do you breed?" asked the driver.

"I breed and train guard dogs. They are mostly German Shepherd, Doberman and Rottweiler. The German Shepherds have the brains, the other two breeds have the looks that people want. I mix them with timber wolves to get the temperament needed in a guard dog."

April lowered her backseat window. "Do they bark all the time?"

"No, only if unannounced strangers come looking around. Remember young lady, these dogs are trained."

"Oh," replied April.

April and Edmond approached the abandoned castle. The path to the castle was overgrown with weeds and small saplings. A Greek had purchased it and spent a considerable amount of money restoring it. New floors and ceilings had been added. He failed, however, to secure the required permission needed for a restoration from the various planning boards and historical societies. Collectively they forced the owner to stop his restoration, leading him to place it on the market. In his disgust, he lowered the asking price far below market value. He was anxious to sell it and return to Greece with whatever money he could get from the sale.

April looked at Edmond. "There is no door. It looks like someone blasted the entryway."

"Probably did, and the devil's name was Oliver

Cromwell," answered the driver who stopped short of the gaping wound. As Richard examined the castle entrance, he said, "I wouldn't give them more than 40,000 euros. Not one cent more."

"April," Edmond said, "the agent told me that one corner of the castle had also been dynamited but it has since been repaired. Years back before Ireland took pride in its past, it was not uncommon for local folks to dynamite castles in order to get the building blocks to use for their fences and to construct their own lodgings."

As Edmond and April walked further into the abandoned ruin, a damp smell permeated the air with the scent of moist stone. After looking at the ground-level storage area, they slowly walked up the winding stone steps to the first floor of the castle. "Be careful," shouted Edmond. "It is dark in here. You nearly fell through a murder hole."

"A what?" asked April.

"A murder hole. It is a small opening through which arrows could be shot down on invaders in the lower level. Very deadly indeed. It rendered the castle highly defensible."

"Thanks for warning me. Next time, do it before I nearly fall through one," she said, laughing.

The second floor contained an arched chapel. Above it was the grand hall with a large medieval fireplace. Open windows looked upon the Gearagh and the River Lee. Straw was scattered on the floor, left by the nesting residents of the windowless castle. Birds flew back and forth from the castle to the meadows and wooded areas that surrounded Fomhoire.

Beautiful wild flowers, including wild angelica, grew nestled among the large ancient trees that led to the River Lee. There the waters sped rapidly, bouncing upon the stones. April stood looking at the river, then turned around. "Edmond, this really is a beautiful place. I think you and I could be happy here on our vacations. I don't think it would take a great deal of effort to make the storage room into a very nice flat. Wouldn't you agree?"

"I agree," said Edmond, buoyed by her enthusiasm. "I am ready to start today."

Upon returning to the car, they announced to Richard that they had decided to buy the castle. He gave them a solemn stare. "There is no point in trying to talk you out of it then. Would if I could, you know. You Yanks are a stubborn lot."

Upon returning to Dublin, they purchased the castle, using their life savings as down payment. Afterwards the Bryants returned to the States so Edmond could finish the semester prior to the summer vacation. In addition, he applied for and received a year's sabbatical. This would give them enough time to renovate the one essential floor of the castle with most of the heavy work allocated to local citizens. The various planning boards and historical societies were happy that someone was willing to restore Fomhoire in compliance with their guidelines. No one mentioned the legends regarding the castle to the Bryants.

In midsummer they moved in. The first few evenings were the most wonderful of their lives. Their adventure was a success. While the improvements turned out to be easier and less expensive than they had anticipated, they decided to renovate only the storage area and nothing more. The remaining four stories of the castle were left as is. April attempted to sweep the upper floors but it proved too great a chore. The dust just seemed to reappear.

To keep out the animals and the uncomfortable draft up the stone stairs, they closed off the upper floors. Rather than replace the castle's heavy door, they chose to place glass in the entrance along with a lightweight metal door that afforded more protection than a modern wooden door would have. As a result, their one main room was filled with natural illumination in the dim light of Ireland. Outside April planted a variety of fruit trees along with many varieties of roses. To protect them from the wind and cold, Edmond restored the partially damaged wall that had at one time surrounded the tower.

The Bryants attempted to make friends with the O'Keef family across the narrow road from them. The woman was friendly enough yet her husband remained distant. Their son stood over six feet tall and was broad of shoulders. As a young man, he was struck in the head by a steel beam that had fallen while his father was building the kennels. He only stared, made a few sounds and remained apart from the family. Even though the dogs barked loudly into the night, Edmond did not complain for the castle walls, being six feet thick, eliminated all ambient sounds from the outside.

In the evenings, they would sit by the peat fire and read. Their lives quickly became one of simplicity. They had no Nooks or Kindles to occupy their time. Their iPad remained in the luggage they had brought from the States. Instead, they read books from the local library or purchased them from used bookshops in Macroom.

All their potable water was pumped from the River Lee. Drinking water was boiled first while untreated water was used for washing and bathing. April preferred dresses that were full length while Edmond wore woolen pants for even the summer was very cool and wet.

April and Edmond had hoped to have children but so far April was unable to become pregnant. They promised each other to get tested when they returned to the States. The fact that she could not become pregnant bothered April. Edmond always assured her that it was probably his low sperm count that was the problem and that diet, medicine or various treatments could eliminate his infertility.

April began to change in late September when the fall flowers started blooming. Already, the topmost leaves of the elms were changing color. She could sense the heavy weight of winter's approach. The days quickly became cloudy, damp and chilly.

Perhaps it was seasonal depression that began to erode her optimism. She no longer smiled nor did she rise early to watch the sun appear above the low hills. Edmond would often return from working in the garden to find her staring; her expression becoming increasingly a blank canvas void of emotion.

April said pleadingly, "Edmond, it would be nice to return to the States for a visit. I miss my home in South Carolina. I long to see my family again."

He did not know how to respond. Edmond was very happy at Fomhoire. It was the fulfillment of his fantasies. He enjoyed role-playing the past in his thoughts. He knew he had no royal forebears or anyone of prominence in his family, he only wished that it were so.

Edmond began to go to Macroom more and more frequently. At first, he went there for building materials and to purchase the necessary tools for woodworking. He had always possessed a love for hand-carved furniture. He wanted to be able to claim that the furniture in Fomhoire was all handmade by him. April was more than willing for him to follow his pursuit since the cheaply made furnishing they now had did not compliment a tower such as theirs.

Gradually Edmond began to frequent the pubs of the small rural town. April talked less and less to him. The verbal intimacies shared between lovers no longer existed. Rarely did they embrace or kiss. Their lovemaking ceased with the approaching fall.

While walking near the edge of the river on one of his frequent visits to Macroom, he noticed a pub that was unusual in its appearance. The outside of The Knight's Errand Inn looked inviting, especially the carved image of a knight in armor looking upon a hardwood castle.

As he entered the pub, the room appeared darker than he had expected. At first, the bartender and patrons just stared at him. They remained silent as he stood at the bar waiting to be served. He could feel their stares penetrating his back. The bartender slowly turned around to acknowledge his presence.

"Sir, I would like a pint of Guinness," Edmond said softly so as not to garner further attention to himself.

"Where are you from in the States?" asked the server of drinks as he filled a glass, tilting it correctly so as to avoid excessive head.

"Is it that obvious I am not local?" he asked, grinning.

"Hell yes," the stocky Irishman replied, his accent strong.

"Well, you are correct, I am a misplaced Yankee. My family is from Connecticut, but my wife's family is from

Charleston."

"A mixed breed," shouted a voice from the back of the room. Every patron of the pub could be heard laughing.

"What are you doing in Macroom?" asked another client. "We are not a tourist stop."

"I bought Castle Fomhoire."

"You did what? Do you have any idea what you have purchased? Typical of a Yank with money to burn," he said as he looked around at the other patrons.

"You arrive uninvited and buy our history," said another gentleman from the shadows of the bar.

"You have nothing to worry about. You see, I bought it from a Greek," replied Edmond.

Those congregated in the bar laughed.

"Come over here and join us with your beer and Yankee dollars," said a young construction worker who had not yet cleaned the sawdust and dried putty from his shirt. "My name is Jess and my friend is John."

"Jess, you implied that I made a mistake buying the castle. I admit it was in ruins and will take a great deal of work and money to make other portions of it livable. You Irish make it difficult for us Yanks to spend money. Our plan to have a john, ah, a toilet installed in the place had to undergo several reviews."

"You are right, Yank. It makes it hard on us workers who need your dollars," said John. "Remember me if you need some work done on the place. Just be sure it is before sundown." With that comment, the two men exchanged smiles.

"You make me feel like the castle is not the friendliest of places. Anything I should know about it?" Edmond asked in a serious tone.

"You might say that. I wouldn't want to spend one night in it. You know what Fomhoire means?"

"Yes, someone explained that to me. It means 'from the sea.'"

John looked at him intently. "Think about it."

"Okay, I give up. What's the joke?" Edmond asked.

"The Formorians were the ancient ancestors of evil fairies and all misshapen men. In our literature, the leprechauns are described as being descendants of the Fomhoire."

Edmond laughed. "That's an old wife's tale, nothing more."

"You know that the waters of the River Lee travel to the sea, right? The question is, what came up *from* the sea to your castle thousands of years before you bought the ground it sits on?" asked John.

"A good sea breeze, I hope." Edmond laughed.

"Laugh if you will. If you are wise, you will leave the castle as soon as you can. Take what anyone will offer you and go back to the States," said Jess, who was quiet up to this point.

"Gentlemen, if you will excuse me, I need to return home. I am sure my wife must be worried about me being so late getting back," said Edmond as he pushed the heavy oak chair away from the table. The men only followed him with their eyes as he left the pub.

As Edmond drove back, he did not pay attention to where he should have turned. The conversation in the pub filled his thoughts. He continued down the one-lane road. "Oh shit," he said out loud. "I forgot to look for my turn off." The road was now too narrow for him to immediately turn around.

Edmond motored on until he saw what appeared to be a drive into the darkening woods. As he turned in, he noticed that the road led to what appeared to be an early Celtic cemetery. Tall Irish crosses, darkened with green moss, clustered in a field under large chestnut and yew trees. Among the graves grew small saplings. The cemetery lay in obvious neglect.

A light rain was beginning to fall as Edmond stopped the car and got out to observe such a beautiful, yet melancholy setting. He found an umbrella in the backseat and went to walk among the graves. The inscriptions were often in Irish, a language that he failed to master even though his scholarly nature dictated that he learn the language of traditional Ireland.

Then he stopped. Among the weathered stones, there was what appeared to be a new one. While the inscription was in Irish, the name of the occupant was easy to read: ABRANYCHUS BACCHIOS ALEXOPOULOS, 1936–2015, OF CASTLE FOMHOIRE.

"That is not possible," said Edmond to himself. "I just bought the castle from him less than six months ago. Why is a Greek with such an unusual name buried in an abandoned Celtic cemetery close to nowhere? It must be a son with the same name, but even that does not make sense." As he stood in thought, the gentle rain striking his umbrella warned him of heavier showers to follow. "I will have to come back here when the weather is more favorable."

As he walked back towards his car, he saw another gravestone that was not adorned with a Celtic Cross: DAME A. P. BRYANT, 1850–1877, WIFE OF SIR EDMOND O'BRYANT, 1845–1877, OF CASTLE FOMHOIRE.

"What a crude, thoughtless joke," he said out loud.

"Someone is playing an elaborate joke on us all. I bet if I look more closely among the graves, I will find my own grave. Sick bastards!" He slammed his car door shut. As he sped towards the gate lodge that led to the burial site, he hit a yew tree near the entrance of the cemetery. Dazed, he looked up at the tree as wet brown leaves began to fall gently about the car like winter snow. He turned towards the cemetery. A woman with white skin and hair the color of flames stood gazing at him. Then all went black.

Edmond awoke, feeling the pain caused by the collision. He felt sticky, drying blood on his forehead. The impact had cracked the front bumper but the car was still drivable. "Thank goodness I took out insurance when I leased the car." Edmond then drove slowly towards Fomhoire, his temper abating.

April saw him through the glass as he approached the front door, his gait unsteady. "What on earth happened to you?" she asked. Her expression aptly bore her concern.

"I had an accident. Somehow I missed the turn to the castle and drove too far down the road. I tried to turn around on a lane that led into an abandoned cemetery. Most of the markers were inscribed in Irish. As I was leaving the cemetery, I looked back and saw something in the woods. That's when I ran into a yew tree. Thank goodness the damage is cosmetic to the car. Somehow I struck my head on something, probably the rearview mirror. I was foolish and failed to properly secure my seatbelt. It was my carelessness that injured me."

"A figure? What do you mean?" she asked.

"I really don't know. I glimpsed movement in my side

mirror and turned to look back. That's when I left the road and hit the tree."

"I am sorry. No matter how careful we intend to be, accidents do happen to us all." She paused. "You look so shaken up. Your hands are even trembling," she said as she washed the blood from his forehead.

"I know I was unconscious for a short time and may have imagined some things, but I want you to come with me to the cemetery. I need to know if what I saw was real."

"Are you certain you want me to go with you now? I think it would be best for you to lie down. That is a nasty gash on your forehead."

"No! We need to leave as soon as possible before it gets darker. I must know what I saw was real," he repeated, feeling slightly dazed.

"What did you see?"

"I saw Abranychus' grave?"

"You saw what?"

"Abranychus' grave."

"That can't be. When we bought the castle he was in Greece, or at least, the auctioneer said he was. He indicated to us all that he was fed up with the red tape that Ireland forces upon outsiders. The last place he would want to be buried is in Ireland. They practically threatened him with deportation in Macroom when he flew into rage after losing his last appeal. Are you sure you did not confuse what the inscriptions said since Irish is such a difficult language to read?"

"That is not true. I know what I read!"

"I hate to repeat myself, but what you read, according to you, was in Irish. You must simply have gotten confused after hitting your head. Besides, all old markers are difficult to read. What led you to think it was a recent grave?"

"It seemed to glisten. I know that does not make sense since it was raining and the sky was obviously darkening. I don't know what made it appear to be luminescent except for being new."

"You see, you really don't have an explanation. It just goes to prove that you were confused at the time, but to make you feel better, I will drive you."

Edmond was silent as April drove their midsize SUV carefully. She was not familiar with the road as it narrowed through the thickening mass of ancient trees that wainscoted the road. The deeper woods began to darken as the fall sun rested uneasily upon the horizon.

April looked towards him. "Edmond, how far did you drive? I have been driving fifteen minutes and you haven't said a word." She continued to look towards Edmond who remained staring out the side window.

"I don't really remember," he replied. "It did not seem like a long time."

"Let's go home," said April reluctantly, realizing how upset Edmond was. It was his wont to lapse into silence whenever he became upset. She turned the car around realizing the futility of their traveling further.

That night the wind blew strongly. It whistled past the doors and whined through each floor of the castle. The clouds shot forth bolts of lightning, but it did not rain. April and Edmond lay still, listening to the intrusion of wind and claps of thunder. Soon the guard dogs across the lane began to howl. They too felt the primitive fear that their wild ancestors had experienced in the deep woods of preglacial Ireland.

Soon Edmond's drowsiness led to sleep. In his dream he returned to the cemetery. There, beneath a large yew tree, stood a beautiful woman. Her hair blew in the strong breeze, her eyes piercing blue. Her skin looked as white and soft as fresh Wicklow snow that sought the boughs of great oaks. As he walked towards her, she extended her hand to him. He held it tightly as they walked to the River Lee. There they disrobed and entered the frigid waters of the river. They looked into each other's eyes. There she wrapped her arms and her legs about him. Suddenly he was being forced beneath the surface of the river. He fought to free himself from her embrace.

"Edmond, Edmond, wake up! You are hurting me," shouted April. Edmond released his grip on her. "You were covering me with your body while, at the same time, tearing us apart. You even ripped my gown!"

"April, I am sorry," he said, rolling over to the other side of the bed. "I was dreaming. Such a real dream. I have never experienced anything even remotely like it before."

He turned away from her, afraid to go to sleep. Slowly the amber-colored light of morning crept into the room. Edmond arose and stood before the narrow window, gazing at the River Lee.

After a breakfast of morning tea and scones, April said, "It's a beautiful day for a swim. It is the first day I can remember that we don't have an overcast sky." She looked at him and smiled.

Meeting her gaze, Edmond said, "I do not need to remind you that fall is already here. The water is far too cold and swimming in it would be dangerous."

"Don't be silly. At least sit on the bank and keep me company."

Edmond reluctantly joined her at the river's edge. The current was flowing swiftly. He admired how beautiful she was to him. Her body sculptured by hours of exercise in various gyms. Even in the castle, she continued to push herself to walk from the lower floor to the top of the castle several times a day. Sometimes even running as though she were being chased. Occasionally he could hear her talking to someone as she ran up the winding stone steps. When he asked her with whom she was conversing, she simply replied, "I was only talking to the wind. Are you jealous of something that cannot be seen?"

"Come on, Edmond, get in the water. You will get used to it quickly. Don't baby yourself so much. How can I admire a man that is so afraid?"

Edmond got off his towel and entered the water, careful not to step on any sharp stones that lined the bottom of the narrow river. He dove underwater and quickly resurfaced. As he looked about, he could not see April. Then he saw a figure further down the fast-moving river.

"April?" he asked. In the distance, her hair appeared different, perhaps altered by the mist that crept over the water. As he swam towards her, she disappeared behind a small island of grass and saplings.

Panic gripped him. Even though he was swimming in her direction, he could not see her. He swam until his arms became heavy weights in the frigid water. He felt a leg cramp coming. Exhausted and trembling from the cold, he swam to a bank made out of piled river stones and continued to yell her name. Only a flight of rising birds returned his loud and fervent pleas.

He ran towards Fomhoire hoping to retrieve his cell phone. He knew that he would need help in finding her. As soon as he reached the castle, he pushed open the door. April was sitting at the coffee table, still in her nightgown. She yawned. "What on earth are you doing? You are dripping wet. Is it raining outside?"

He stared at her as his heart rate returned to normal. Legs trembling, he sagged into the chair opposite hers. "How can you be in your nightgown? We were just swimming in the river and you vanished!"

"Edmond, promise me that you will see a doctor. You must have hallucinated, and I am very worried about you. By the time I finished my walk on the tower steps, you were gone. I looked everywhere but didn't find you."

Edmond agreed to see a doctor in Cork. A psychologist named Kevin McKinney was recommended by a member of the historical society that had earlier approved their work on the castle. Since he suffered from depression in the States, April insisted that he obtain the name of a doctor in Ireland. Edmond, however, felt that it was foolish to see one since he was certain he would get better in time. He felt that the task of rebuilding the tower had only fatigued him both mentally and physically.

After filling out copious forms, he was led by the psychologist's secretary down a dimly lit hallway to a large oaken door. After knocking, she stepped back, allowing him to enter. "Good morning, Dr. McKinney. My name is Edmond Bryant. A member of the County Cork Historical Association recommended you."

The doctor rose to greet him. "It is my pleasure to meet you, Edmond. I was told I might expect a call from you." He paused. "I know Mrs. Cunningham very well. She is my second cousin's daughter. A fine woman. What seems to be the concern?"

"My wife insisted that I see a psychologist. I don't think I really need one."

"If you truly believed that, you would not have come. Men, once they make their own diagnosis, can indeed be a very stubborn lot."

Edmond looked straight at the psychologist for the first time. He noticed that Dr. McKinney avoided eye contact with him. It immediately struck Edmond that the doctor could be autistic. In addition, he was a bald, middle-aged man who was so overweight he needed to gulp air with each sentence. His frayed vest supported a large gold watch, reminiscent of the kind his own grandfather used to wear.

"Please tell me about what has brought you here."

"I related several events to April, my wife, that I must admit are peculiar in nature. I saw a person in a cemetery that may not exist. I shouldn't say that or you will think I am mad. I should have said that I saw a very unusual person in a burial ground."

"Unusual?"

"Yes, that is the case. Her appearance even her clothing was atypical of what you might expect to see in a rural cemetery. I can only tell you that she was there and that she was real. As real as you are."

"An unusual woman in a cemetery is not uncommon at all. Often when we lose a mate, we dress differently, appear differently. I am sure that what you saw was simply a local woman visiting the grave of a loved one. You must have startled her."

"I saw other things in the cemetery that disturbed me as well. What I saw I cannot explain on any rational level."

"So, your wife believes that you see things that are not there?"

"My wife does not believe me, but I did not hallucinate. What I experienced is very real."

"To you, at least," commented Dr. McKinney. "Is there a common theme that runs throughout your experiences?"

"Yes, cold flowing water and dimming winter light frequently appear in my dreams," Edmond responded. He was reluctant to mention the inscriptions on the two graves.

"Well, in Ireland, those are things we take for granted."

"In the form you completed, you said that you live on the River Lee near Macroom. I am somewhat familiar with that area. My uncle had a small pub there in the 60s. When I was young, my mother and I would visit the village. Tell me, where exactly is your house? You failed to write down the address."

"Doctor, I don't think I can refer to my dwelling as a house. You see, it is a fifteenth-century tower castle."

"Now don't tell me, it's not Castle Fomhoire, is it? I

heard about the troubles that the Greek had in restoring it. Something to do with not obtaining the proper permits."

"Yes, it is. My wife and I love living there. At least, I am not hallucinating about that."

"I heard it was for sale. It is rare that a place like that ever sells. If it does, it quickly goes right back on the market. People that buy castles are usually not very realistic about what it takes to restore and maintain such a structure." He paused. "There are many stories about that castle. Of course, they are just stories."

"What kind of stories?" asked Edmond.

"Oh, just events fed by superstitions, or you might say, hauntings."

"Please tell me more about these so-called hauntings."

"We should not discuss such things during your first session. We must focus on your wellbeing. A discussion that relates to the supernatural can only make your condition worse. Besides, there are no definite answers to the questions that come up from such talks. We bring our own prejudices and preconceived opinions to any such discussion. An atheist and a spiritual person see things quite differently, but it is in our nature to doubt."

Edmond knew he was the patient and not the doctor. The psychologist meant to lead him down a carefully orchestrated path. He knew he was becoming increasingly disturbed by the events that had transpired. "What normal man sees apparitions?" he asked himself. "There is but one world, and it consists only of that which can be seen, heard, touched, tasted and smelled. All else is but a longing for a reason to exist. A purpose behind finding ourselves in a void of unfulfilled desires."

Edmond left Cork feeling depressed. He was given prescriptions for nothing more than sleeping pills and Valium. He knew he would eventually be given more specific medication for whatever illness, if any, possessed him.

Upon his arrival at the castle, an alarmed April opened the door. As soon as he entered, she locked it by sliding the security bar across it.

"April, what is wrong? I have never seen you so scared. Your hands are trembling."

"Edmond, I was doing the dishes when I felt someone staring at me. I know that everyone has had that sensation before but this feeling was very intense. I turned around and there beyond the glass was the dog owner's son. He was staring at me. His appearance was frightening. He just stood there with his dark sunken eyes and wild black hair. His eyes spoke an intense emotion – one of dislike, perhaps even hatred."

"How long did he remain there?"

"I don't know. I closed the shutters and locked myself in the bathroom. Outside the window, I could hear someone walking through the brambles, stopping, and then walking again. After that I waited for you to return."

"April, don't be afraid. It has to be that we are strangers to him. Being mentally challenged, he does not know how to place us in his unstructured thoughts. Like when encountering a wild animal, just walk away while facing him. Whatever you do, do not say anything to him or run. He is probably functioning on primeval instinct, one where pursuit is fundamental to survival."

"I am thankful that you rebuilt the corner stone wall. I will try to keep the garden gate locked when you are not here."

"From now on, I will just ring the bell whenever I return. I know it is primitive but you should be able to hear the bell when you are inside," said Edmond in an attempt to calm her fears.

Edmond looked more closely at her. "I noticed that you have not been sleeping soundly either. Has anything else been bothering you?"

"Yes, I didn't want to mention it, but the other day I went to the chapel. While I was taking the stairs for exercise, I thought I heard someone or something in there. When I entered the chapel, I noticed that Saint Brigit's cross above the stone altar was missing. I haven't been in there in days. It sort of creeps me out that someone would take or even move it."

"I am sure we will find it. Probably one of the village women we hired to sweep and clean the castle removed it, perhaps to polish it. You know that kind of metal requires polishing or else it tarnishes. I love how the setting sun reflects off of it. It looks like gold on fire."

"I don't believe they would have been able to reach it. It is too heavy to take down," said April.

"I agree with you about the weight. I can't believe it was forged from iron, then dipped in gold-like metal. I have no idea what kind. The cross must weigh seventy-five pounds or more."

That night he dreamed of the woman he had briefly seen. He knew that she was only a figment of his imagination or the product of his illness. Perhaps she was a longing that he was attempting to define. Her red hair and piercing eyes could not escape him. Her full-length white dress flowed behind her, billowing in the wind that moved through a backdrop of yew and chestnut trees. She appeared exactly as he had seen her in the cemetery.

Edmond tossed and turned until he awakened. He felt for April, but she was not there. He immediately rose to put on his robe and started up the stone stairs. When he reached the second floor of the tower, he noticed that all of the candles on the chapel altar had been lit. The sweet smell of incense clung to the air. St. Brigit's Cross was once more on the stone wall exactly where it was when they had purchased the castle.

There, kneeling before the altar was the woman from the woods. She was adorned in the white gown, her red hair hung about her neck. Edmond remained motionless. The stone beneath her body appeared wet. The moisture clinging to her body began to turn to blood as she smiled at him.

Suddenly, Edmond awoke from the dream. He was soaked in his own sweat. He sat up and looked at April, who was sleeping soundly next to him. He knew inwardly that it was he who was changing, not her as he had previously thought.

The day was unusually cool. The steady rain threatened to continue throughout the afternoon and night. They ate their meal in constrained silence, both thinking about the other. It was as though they had adorned cloaks and made themselves invisible to the one they loved.

"Edmond, it is probably going to rain all afternoon and into the evening. Would you object if I went to the library in Macroom? There might be some interesting new novels out. I might also see what DVDs are available. There is a movie that

I've been waiting to see."

"What movie is that?" he questioned.

"You know that I am a fan of Jessica Chastain. She stars in *Miss Julie*. It is based on a story written in 1888."

"Sure, but give me a call when you start back. As you know, these roads can be treacherous in the dark."

"Treacherous? Oh, come now. Be realistic. We are living our dream in a most beautiful place. There is no more danger here than there was in Boston. The question is, will you be alright while I am gone?"

"Of course," he said, looking towards the walled garden.

She dressed warmly for the rain had brought a chill to the wind. She regretted that soon the River Lee would be much too cold for their relaxing afternoon swim. It was their special time together. There they would express their own emotions and satisfy their natural urges as man and woman.

After she drove away, Edmond went outside to the garden and sat on a chaise lounge, one of the few unnecessary luxuries they had purchased. He closed his eyes as he sought the warmth of the still air behind the wall that separated the castle from the guard dogs of the neighbor. Soon he became chilled and decided to walk down the lane that led past the site of a house in ruins built by the British ascendancy class. The new owners of the land had neglected it and then, after removing the roof to save on property taxes, allowed the rafters and timbers to fall to the basement below. Eventually, they removed the stone, using it to build themselves a house and to create the stone walls that served as boundary.

Edmond stopped and looked at the few walls that remained of such former splendor. He imagined the great parties and pleasures of the reigning class before the land acts and troubles. Had Fomhoire been easy to destroy, it too would have been torched. Instead it was allowed to remain roofless with the floors eventually collapsing upon themselves; a habitat of wild animals and river birds.

Then he looked back at the castle that was beginning to be lost in the dying twilight. As he started walking back, the guard dogs began to bark loudly. He could hear them hitting the walls of their cages. He knew that if any dog had been set free, it would attack him out of instinct and from the cruel training they had received. A pack of dogs would be deadly.

As he walked past the metal cages, the tall stout figure of the trainer's son stood among the pens. It was as though he might release the dogs at any minute. He knew that because of the brain injury, no court would convict him of murder. Edmond did not look in his direction but walked quickly past.

He entered the darkening castle door as it squeaked upon it hinges. The musty smell had returned, an odor of dampness. He usually removed his boots when entering, but this time he did not. Edmond sensed that he needed to remain dressed yet there was no apparent reason for his uneasiness.

He could not help but become sleepy even though the light of the dimming sun still touched the castle rooms. He added additional peat to the fire that burned with a warm glow. Intending to remain awake until April returned, he fixed himself a cup of Irish breakfast tea, his favorite.

As he looked at the pendulum of the parlor clock, his eyes closed. Suddenly he heard a scream from one of the upper floors. He jumped to his feet, throwing the quilt off as he ran towards the entryway to the stone stairway. Swiftly he checked the chapel and continued to the third floor where the great hall was located. There he saw April dripping wet as though she had returned from the river. She stared at him.

"April! What on earth are you doing here? Why didn't you let me know you had returned?"

"I arrived just a few moments ago. I noticed light coming from the great hall. I thought you were up here so I wanted to be with you."

"Why are you so wet?"

"It has been pouring outside. I forgot my umbrella."

"Has the river been rising?"

"Yes, not only rising but flowing rapidly. At the library, they said that the rains could continue for awhile, maybe even days."

"Tell me again, why are you in the great hall?"

"Like I just told you, I saw light from below as I was driving up," repeated April.

Edmond glanced at her. "I heard a scream just after I fell asleep. I didn't know what to think. I feared that you were in danger."

April looked at Edmond. "I see that you have a flashlight. What I saw was more like a small torch burning."

"Well, I can assure you that all I have is a flashlight. I think now that what I heard was an owl or perhaps a nesting hawk. Since I was asleep, I can't be sure of what I heard," said Edmond.

They then walked down the stone stairs to the lower floor of the castle. "Tell me, April, what did you read in the library. Anything about Fomhoire?"

"As a matter of fact, yes. I made a copy of the page that

was referenced by an article on historical estates of Ireland. It is from the county newspaper." April unfolded the copy.

Cork Examiner. Edward Penson. September 11, 1936.

Tragedy once more struck at Fomhoire Castle. The body of the estate owner's wife, Lady Bryant, was found by a local hunting party Thursday afternoon. Since the possibility of wolves was ruled out, the wounds found on Lady Bryant's body appear to have been made by a large dog or dogs.

Fomhoire was the site of a similar accident in October 1923, when the estate owner, Baron Bryant, father of Philip Bryant, discovered that his wife had been killed by an Irish wolfhound that belonged to the Baron. Baron Bryant attributed the unprovoked attack on his wife as an accident due to the volatile nature of the breed.

Irish wolfhounds are bred to attack bears and other large marauding animals such as wild boar. It is rare, however, for them to be aggressive towards people, especially when they have been raised as pets. The Baron, however, had the dog trained to be a watch dog and to be aggressive towards intruders.

I did further search on the Internet and found an additional reference to Fomhoire Castle in connection with castles and Irish myths. It seems like our castle is not as friendly as we have previously thought. In the early 1500s, the lord of the estate suspected his wife of adultery with one of the house servants. Even though both she and her supposed lover denied their relationship, they were let go only to be pursued by the lord's hunting dogs. It seems that in his fit of insane jealousy, he turned the whole matter into a sporting event."

"I can't believe the similarities between the three events that have happened at the castle," he replied.

"Edmond, it really bothers me that the fellow just across the lane trains watch dogs. I am getting a little afraid to even walk down to the river."

"April, don't worry. Remember that his dogs are kept in metal cages. Besides they are instructed to obey commands and are also taught not to injure unless given very specific instructions."

"It still bothers me," April said as she prepared to lie down for the evening.

They both lay in bed with their eyes open, staring at the silhouettes cast by the fire on the timber beams above them. Before Edmond realized it, morning had come. He could hear the guard dogs barking loudly as sunlight entered the room. Outside the brilliant red of late Irish roses could be seen.

"April, are you asleep?" She did not answer. "April!" There was no reply. He glanced about the room. He sensed that something unusual must have occurred. Edmond quickly dressed and went to check each floor of the castle, panting as he ascended the almost vertical stone steps. Still he could not find

April.

Edmond had an overpowering feeling that she had gone for a morning swim in the river. A sensation of awareness that he could not explain.

He left the castle and hurried down to the river. The water was rising rapidly, inching up the trunks of the trees that clung to the riverbank. He waded chest deep into the cold water, calling her name repeatedly. There was no reply. As he waded back towards the shore, he slipped. The ice-cold water held him in its grip until he could swim. He had apparently stepped into a deep hole in the riverbed. A depression that he did not know existed.

Edmond left the water and hurried towards the road. He then ran down the lane that bordered the River Lee. As he jogged, he heard the barking of the guard dogs. He kept glancing at the rapidly flowing waters that paralleled the lane. When he rounded a bend in the road, he saw the son of the dog trainer. He was standing in the middle of the road holding two Irish wolfhounds. The two large dogs barked aggressively, straining against their chains. With each leap of the dogs, he further released his grip. Edmond stopped and waited for the attack. As the dogs lunged towards him, the son of the dog keeper blew a small whistle that he held in his mouth. Instantly the two dogs stopped just short of him and sat on their haunches, fur raised, ears pointing backwards. Both continued to emit deep growls.

Edmond backed away from the dogs. Moving forward could only be interpreted as a challenge to which they were more than capable of responding to.

The keeper of the dogs smiled as he retreated. As much

as he wanted to make a run for the castle, Edmond walked slowly backwards so as not to act like a prey and rouse the dogs' instinct to give chase.

Once in the safety of the castle, Edmond raced once more up the stairs to each of the tower floors, but April was nowhere to be found.

After being notified, the police conducted searches along the banks of the river and into the Gearagh, its banks lined with submerged trees. Bloodhounds traced her walk into the river but could not reestablish a trail.

A later inquiry ruled April's death to be probable drowning. After six months, the case was closed and April was declared legally dead. With the rise of the river and its rapid flow, her body had, in the opinion of the police, been swept out to sea.

Nightly Edmond waited for her return. Only the sounds of the forest and the wind were his companions. He put the castle on the market but there were no takers. He seldom saw the keeper of the dogs. Occasionally, he would see his son walking various attack breeds down the lane. Edmond withdrew from the community and lived as though the castle was under siege.

The estate of April's mother finally paid for the castle. In that Edmond now possessed what then remained of her inheritance, he was financially able to wait for a sale. At the back of his mind, he kept hoping that April would reappear or that a sighting of her would occur. Occasionally he would hear someone mention seeing an attractive young red-headed woman sitting on the bank of the river.

Questions kept racing through his mind. Why would she get up in the night and bathe in the river? He knew she was not depressed, or so he reasoned, enough to take her own life.

Who was the mysterious woman that he had seen in the burial ground? Later he searched for the burial ground but could not locate it. All he found in its place was a grove of ancient oak trees. April had convinced him that he was hallucinating, or at best, dreaming. Was there a connection between this woman, Fomhoire and April's disappearance?

Shortly thereafter, Edmond returned to the States to pursue what remained of his life.

Chapter 2
LOOKING FOR ANN PENNINGTON

In the dim light of his study, Edmond Bryant's Blackberry notified him that he had just received an e-mail. It read, "Ann Pennington wants to be friends with you on Facebook" – a simple message that he too frequently ignored. After all, he had over 1,400 unknown friends already on Facebook. At first, it was fun adding the anonymous to his list. He had grown weary, however, after he had received some requests from less than desirable people who sought only to appeal to his prurient interest. In the past, if a person wanted to be a friend, he would confirm their request without even looking up their Facebook page. Now he made it a habit to invite only those with whom he shared a common interest or who flattered his ego.

However, the name "Ann Pennington" seemed strangely familiar to him. He could not recall where he might have met her. Perhaps it was at a faculty club party. She might have even been one of his students. After all, he was a nice-looking professor of classical languages. His classes were inevitably small when he was first appointed as an associate professor. Before long he was well known on the Ivy League campus. Due to his popularity, the administration had to relocate his introductory classes to a larger lecture hall every semester.

His lectures combined scholarship with theatrics. As he addressed the class, he would toss his long black hair whenever he wished to emphasize a point. At times he would race towards his hardback chair, mount it and talk from the added height of his oratorical position.

It was a Friday night, a night that he now dreaded. In the past, he and April would schedule a dinner date together, a small festive event to celebrate nothing more than not having to get up early the next morning. When she first vanished, his friends had invited him out of respect for April but that soon ended. His phone no longer rang after he made it very clear that he had no intention of remarrying or even dating. April's presence was still too strong for him to let her go. She continued to dwell in his thoughts and dreams. He spent much of his evenings contemplating the possibilities of her death.

Ireland was to be a new beginning for them both. He had repressed so many thoughts regarding their relationship. On purchasing their first small starter house in a community of commuters and scholars, their relationship had began to change. At first, they enjoyed working in the yard together and even collecting antiques at various yard sales. Almost imperceptibly they talked less and less. The more time he devoted to his work and the house, the farther apart they seemed to become.

One evening he had worked later in the yard than intended. It was early spring and the yard smelled of roses and honeysuckle. Edmond could sense the enchantment of all that grew within the small garden.

As he approached the house, he heard his wife's voice speaking softly on the phone. As he began to walk up the steps, she suddenly hung up. He thought he heard her say, "I love you, too," but he could not be sure. He wanted to ask her who had called but hesitated, perhaps afraid of the answer.

It bothered him that even though they were married, she continued to stare intensely at men while in his presence. She seemed captivated by even the smile of a stranger. Since she was very beautiful, men would inevitably stare back at her, ignoring the fact that she was with her husband. It was apparent to even the most casual of observers that she was openly seeking someone else.

Even though Edmond confronted her about her flirtatious nature, she denied his allegations. She simply dismissed his concern by saying, "What am I to do – ignore the fact that other people find me attractive?" Soon he accepted her coquettish nature as a part of their relationship.

Edmond felt that if they moved away, their relationship would improve. Even if it meant giving up the house he had grown to love, they might be able to rediscover some degree of passion in their marriage. The money from the sale could be used for trips abroad or to the Caribbean. He also realized that moving away from the campus would separate her from both her friends and the men whose attention she so desired. Deep down, however, Edmond realized that jealousy did not die but only lay dormant.

While they were in Ireland, April's mother died, making her the sole heir of her estate. An inheritance that consisted of a savings account and a large house in the historical district of Charleston. It was to this house that Edmond relocated for the remainder of his sabbatical.

In the months that followed her disappearance, Edmond would sit in her father's study, staring at the chair that April's mother used to rock her in. At times he could see it rock, but then, it was only the wind as it traveled though the large den of the 19th-century Charleston house. There was no way he could afford to keep such a house while living and working in another state. He knew that he needed to sell the house quickly, but found that he could not let it go. It was as though April were still present to disapprove.

Edmond used Facebook as a promotional tool for his novels and artwork – hobbies that he had grown to feel passionate about. He did not provide the visitor with any personal information or a reason to follow him. His Timeline was lifeless and static in nature.

The following day he received a note on his Blackberry stating that he and Ann Pennington were now friends. He knew he had not sent her an invitation. He immediately searched her name. There was an actress named Ann Pennington but she had died on November 4, 1971. He admired the early photograph of her. Ann was small in statue with beautiful red hair. Her Facebook page, however, had been "automatically generated based on what Facebook users are interested in…" It struck him as odd that a person, though dead, could have a Facebook page.

"This shows that even Facebook can screw up," he thought out loud.

Edmond Bryant had earlier published a novel entitled *Lost Graves* based on his personal experiences living in an early 19th-century farmhouse and an antebellum cottage that he had briefly owned prior to his marriage to April. Because of this, he had no desire to publish another ghost story. He did not see himself as a devotee of the macabre. He sought a life that was predictable, a realm of calm in which to immerse himself.

Edmond's book sales had been miserable. He thought, "Perhaps it is fortunate that so few people have been exposed to my writings that are far from scholarly in nature." Writing was his pastime, his escape from a life that he no longer enjoyed. Ever since the assumed death of his wife, his zest for life had ceased. He often described himself as a "dead scholar walking." Perhaps this was true. His whole adult life had revolved around April. She alone gave meaning to his research and later to his creative writing. She, like the female garden spider, had been beautiful, enchanting and deadly to her mate. Love mingled with jealousy continued to stalk its prey.

A week later, he received another notification that simply stated, "Ann Pennington added a photo with you." He searched his own page, but found no photo from her. That evening he received another message: "Ann Pennington tagged you in a photo on Facebook." Another search turned up empty.

"At least I have an admirer, one that does not exist," he said with ironic bitterness.

Soon five years had passed since his return to the States. His reputation as a brilliant scholar had begun to decline. Fewer students registered for his once overcrowded classes.

In his mailbox at work was a handwritten note from the dean: "Dr. Bryant, please call my secretary to arrange a meeting with me." In the academic world such brief notes were not welcome. They could mean only one of two things – a favor to be asked or a criticism to be offered.

After the meeting was arranged, Edmond sat uncomfortably in the secretary's office awaiting the dean's summons. He studied the imitation Van Gogh that added color to the drab off-white wall. Then the secretary motioned him to enter his superior's office.

"Edmond," said his department chair, "what you need is a vacation. I know that you will not take an extended leave even though you've earned it, but a couple of weeks off can't hurt you or your publication record which, by the way, is not as extensive as it should be. You have been through too much during the last few years. You need some time to get your thoughts in order, maybe even share a smile or two with someone. As you know, Sheila and I just got back from a Caribbean cruise. We had a great time!" He smiled. "Visited places that were just as romantic as their names implied. In spite of yourself, you might have fun. You know the F word never hurt anyone."

After a pause, Edmond replied, "Jack, you might be right. April and I had planned such a cruise in the Caribbean just before..." He looked away filled with emotion. Small tears glistened in the light of the office window.

That evening, Edmond sat alone as he repeatedly stirred the

sugar in his cup of coffee. He realized that he could not escape the question that haunted him the most: Is she dead or did she leave him for a lover that may or may not exist? "Whatever the answer," he told himself, "I pray that I will have closure."

As he lifted his spoon from the cup, he took a pen and began to make a checklist for the trip.

Chapter 3
CRUISE TO THE ISLANDS

In celebration of their anniversary, April and Edmond had planned a trip to the Caribbean. They wanted to take a tour of the southern Caribbean islands. As a result they intended to fly to Puerto Rico, spend the night in San Juan and then board a ship the next afternoon. April and her travel agent had planned the trip in detail well ahead of time to ensure few, if any, inconveniences. The goal was to relax, with no timetables to follow, in the pleasure of each other's company.

Edmond decided to follow the same itinerary. As he traveled to the Atlanta airport, he began to question the wisdom of his decision. It was in this moment of indecision that he had a strange sensation. He felt that April was to be with him on the trip. As he entered the terminal, he whispered, "I love you."

The trip to Puerto Rico did not require him to use the International Terminal. He was familiar with domestic flights since his university required that he travel frequently to conferences. After a whiskey sour at a restaurant, he waited with the other passengers who, like him, were tourists headed for Puerto Rico and the cruise ships that arrived and departed from its harbor.

The plane left the tarmac and was soon at cruising altitude. Edmond glanced out the window towards the sea 30,000 feet below, but the glare was too brilliant for him to see the turbulent swells.

The seat next to him was occupied by a young woman who was traveling to join her parents on a cruise. She admitted being apprehensive about flying.

"I understand," said Edmond. "There is so much unpleasant news going around. I think that it increases our anxiety about everything." She did not reply but only clutched her unopened book.

The roar of the engines provided a white noise that soothed him. His eyes felt heavy. He managed to stay awake long enough for the flight attendant to serve him red wine. Then, seduced by the need for sleep, his eyes closed. He saw himself and April on a tropical beach. A place of warm sand and gentle surf. Behind them were large wild coconut palms, their fronds moving in the air. In the distance, smoke rose from some distant source. He could smell the scent of sulfur in the air. April appeared to be wading in the shallow waters as the waves softly lapped at her legs. He swam towards her as she waved to him. Volcanic ash began to fall like large flakes of snow.

Suddenly, the plane bounced as it touched down in San Juan. He waited for the crowd of passengers to rise and gather their carry-ons. He was in no hurry since the *Caribbean Sea Quest* did not sail until the following afternoon.

He arrived at the San Juan Old Town Inn. In the lobby, guests waited in line to check in while their children sat in the few chairs and couches that lined the walls. A large security guard in a sport jacket guarded the entrance to the casino near the entryway. The sound of Latin music permeated the foyer of the large hotel.

Soon a staff member led him to his suite and opened the door. The accommodation was excellent in that it consisted of three rooms wrapped around the seventh floor of the hotel. The view included the harbor from which his ship was scheduled to sail. Having arrived early, he had no reason not to visit the neighboring Old San Juan district.

As he walked up the incline towards the Spanish fort, his footsteps on the cobblestone street sounded loudly. The crowds that had filled the narrow streets soon dispersed as they left work. The air was warm and humid, causing small beads of sweat to gather on his forehead. He paused and wiped the perspiration with his handkerchief. As he stood there, he felt April's presence. It was as though she was waiting for him in one of the numerous shops that lined the streets. He did not see crowds of tourists. Edmond felt very alone as he walked aimlessly about.

As he peered up the street, he saw a woman's face behind a window of antique glass. Her red hair reflected the glow of the setting sun. The distance was too great for him to distinguish her other features. Then she was gone, leaving him with his thoughts of April.

As he began to ascend the bridge that led to the fort, he stopped. Instead he stared at the Atlantic that pounded against the rocks below him. The reefs just off the beach broke the larger waves creating halos of water in the setting sun. In the distance, he could see merchant ships steaming to the various ports of the world. He noticed a beautiful Spanish girl nearby but she did not acknowledge his presence with her eyes nor did she speak.

As the shadows gathered, he enjoyed a very strong margarita from a nearby Mexican restaurant. A beautiful young Latin woman entered the restaurant and seated herself near him but did not look in his direction. From her short, too-tight black dress and makeup, she was obviously a woman who used her charms to seduce men into spending their money. Unlike the other Latin woman he had seen at a distance, she looked at him and smiled. He did not acknowledge her invitation yet he was keenly aware of her presence.

Upon returning to his hotel, he ordered a rum punch at the bar and then sat alone. He carried his tablet with him and wanted to write, but no meaningful thought manifested. He stared at his keyboard as the hands of the restaurant clock moved silently above him. Moisture ran down his drink and pooled about the base of his computer.

He lay on the high thread-count sheets and stared at the paddle fan above him. Outside the sounds of the city could be heard. He was somewhat startled by the loud street noises from the front of the hotel. There was laughter and shouting. He regretted not taking Spanish in college for he longed for the gayety manifested in the music and laughter of the crowd.

He fell asleep far too quickly and awoke from the

dreamless night. He arose sluggishly and prepared to leave the hotel. After concluding the express checkout, he gathered his luggage and saw a red-headed woman who, from a distance, looked like April staring at him. She was motionless for a moment as though she too was trying to identify him. Then she waved. Suddenly she was absorbed by the crowds merging on the narrow sidewalk. He knew it was only someone that looked very much like her.

The driver dropped him off in front of the cruise ship terminal where a large unorganized crowd of vacationers was beginning to form. Before long he was in his stateroom, anxiously awaiting the delivery of his luggage. He had packed his iPad in his oversized suitcase, desiring to use it instead of his laptop. Regardless of what technology he used, he would not have known what to do with his free time without a keyboard present.

After the rituals of farewell, the ship was soon underway. He sat on his balcony watching San Juan's Old Town pass from view. Like the night before, he could hear a celebration coming from the crowded park. It was the sound of Latin music, the type that enticed a person to move their hips freely with the rhythm and to celebrate the gifts of life. He imagined dark eyes flashing as full skirts swirled to the rapid beat.

He sat on his small veranda and looked at the lights of a ship that had departed earlier as she changed course. His ship, *Caribbean Sea Quest*, began a gentle roll. In the darkness, he peered out onto the open ocean. The sky was dark and moonless. The spray from the ocean swells added a salt odor to the night.

Having forgotten to eat lunch, he soon became hungry.

The opulent dining room reserved for his travel class was beautiful compared to the plainness of his life. The servers came from around the world. Each wore a nametag with their country of origin on it. Every need was anticipated and waited upon.

In the presence of the sommelier, he sniffed the bouquet of the wine and nodded for it to be poured.

"Have you sailed with us before?" asked the server of wine.

"Yes, once. But it was a long time ago. My wife and I spent our honeymoon on this very ship. What I remembered most about *Caribbean Sea Quest* was the impeccable service. Our every want was attended to. After we returned home, we made plans for our next voyage on your ship. " He looked towards their favorite table trying not to recall too deeply the love and passion within her eyes. The feeling that he had earlier possessed that life would be an endless journey of pleasures.

"Will your wife be joining you for dinner, sir?" ask the newly arrived food server.

"No, I am afraid that she died five years ago." Even though her death was not confirmed, he felt that his acceptance of it would eventually bring a closure to the wound that would not heal.

"Oh, I am so sorry," replied the food server.

"Thank you. Death is something you never get used to. It is so aberrant. I know that biologically we are programmed to live a finite amount of time, but why? What purpose does death serve the living?"

"Sir, I am only a wardroom server. I cannot answer a question of that depth. Perhaps you should turn to your faith for comfort."

"I have none," Edmond replied.

That evening he ordered duck steeped in an excellent sauce. He also requested asparagus and creamed potatoes. The duck was very good, not stringy as he had encountered in restaurants ashore. The Castello di Ama wine tasted exceptionally good to the palette. Every time his glass was near empty, it was filled once more.

A young couple sat next to his table. The woman wore a black fitted skirt with a matching blouse of silk and had green eyes. She was exquisitely beautiful. A black shawl, typical of those purchased in the finer shops of Turkey, was draped around her shoulders. Even though Edmond was uncomfortable with being so close to their table, he could hear their conversation.

"I am so glad we went to Montserrat," said the man, who had blue eyes and thick black hair.

"Me too," his companion replied. "I loved the beach and the thrill of being near such a dangerous volcano. It was the kind of experience that you only read about. We were so fortunate that the wind did not blow the sulfur fumes and the accompanying ash towards us. The fumes always remind me of my freshmen chemistry class. Yuk!" She paused. "The part that I love best was meeting such interesting people. Ann and I became friends quickly. She is so gorgeous with her red hair and small frame. She looks almost like a child. Of course, my husband noticed her first," she said, smiling at him.

"Well, Punesa, how could I not help but stare? She might as well have been wearing nothing with what she had on. You know, Montserrat, unlike St. Maarten, does not allow public nudity on the beach. After the volcano explosion that destroyed roughly half of their island, they became more puritanical. That conditioning of the soul seems to always follow a tragedy."

"Can you imagine recovering from a violent hurricane only to experience the eruption of a volcano?" Punesa said as she glanced away from her companion towards the stranger who sat across from them.

Edmond turned his head towards their table. "Please excuse me, but I could not help but hear your conversation. I vaguely remember reading something about that island. I believe that it was in the 50s when the volcano first erupted, burying the inhabitants of the capital in lava, and it has been active every since. Geologists are expecting a major eruption at any time. I can't believe people still go to that island. I am too cautious a person to tempt the indifference of nature."

The young husband responded, "Oh, excuse me, my name is Eric and this is my wife, Punesa. I am a biologist at a university. We went there not as tourists but to study the rebirth of the island. We are interested in the rate that the native vegetation returns and what, if any, alien hosts move in. It is a real opportunity for non-native plants to flourish."

"Please don't take offense at my comment. I just realize how precious life is and what great value we should all place on it." Edmond turned away from the couple and looked out the large observation glass towards the ocean with its caps of white and distant clouds that clung to islands without names.

"I am so sorry to bother you again," said Edmond. "Did you happen to catch the name of the young woman that you saw there? I thought I heard you say 'Ann'. Of course, I might have been mistaken."

Punesa smiled once more. "Are you kidding? No way I was going to let my husband introduce himself to her. She was too beautiful and he couldn't have resisted her abundantly displayed charms. She said that her name was Ann. You know that is a very common name."

Eric returned the smile. "Forgive my wife. You would think that I was handsome and a prize for every woman we meet. I appreciate her confidence in me as a lover, but I cannot live with such an illusion of myself."

Edmond asked, "Was the woman short, tall, lean or overweight?"

Punesa replied, "Why are you so interested in a woman that you do not know?"

Edmond paused and then answered, "I knew a red-headed woman in college who mentioned that she loved to travel throughout the islands of the Caribbean. I know it sounds crazy, but I thought it might be her." Edmond felt that the truth was not relevant in the unusual quest that he had set himself upon.

"Well, there are probably several red-headed women on the island. It is called the Emerald Isle since the Irish migrated there many years ago. Of course, the population is largely black but they make a big deal out of the Irish thing. So you see, she might not have been a tourist but a resident," said Punesa.

She then added, "You see the native inhabitants commercializing on the Irish theme when you enter the markets on the island. You know, ashtrays with four-leaf clovers on them. With the ongoing volcanic eruptions, I don't think many Irish will want to live there now. You know, all residents are qualified to immigrate to England. Still, something keeps the remaining three or four thousand there. Of course, the rain and almost constant cloud cover in England don't exactly encourage anyone to stay. It is certainly much more beautiful in Montserrat. Just about anything grows there. I have never seen such beautiful bougainvillea anywhere in the world. The breadfruit trees are also the largest that we have seen in any of the other islands. I really love their lime juice. At one time they were a major exporter of limes."

"My wife even likes the blue butterfly bushes, the island's unwelcome new guests. They have beautiful blue flowers but are known to crowd out the native species," said Eric as he smiled at his wife.

Edmond found it pleasant to have two people willing to penetrate his loneliness. Any companionship was welcome. As he looked out the large window, he thought about their encounter with the strange woman who might be the same one who had friended him on Facebook. Of course, he reasoned, this was just a fantasy; something for him to ponder during the long hours he faced alone.

As he finished his meal, he thought about the women that he knew were single. The desperate women at church that would flock around any single man. He knew a man at his former place of worship that had also become a widower at a relatively young age. Harold had found himself having to engage in conversations with women that he had little or nothing in common with. Their years of being divorced or widowed showed in their lack of care regarding their appearances. What folly to think that love can be found in casual conversations following a discussion of heaven and hell. Harold mentioned to Edmond that he had thought about changing churches simply to avoid hurting their feelings. Of course, the last time Edmond saw Harold at church, his resolve had weakened. Perhaps the desperation of others is a better companion than solitude.

In a sense, Edmond missed being pursued by desperate women. Since April's disappearance, he had not dated nor had any woman sought his companionship. At least dating would validate that he was still of value to someone. Then he paused. No self-pity, he thought, not today.

After leaving the Caribbean Room, Edmond went to the closest ship bar and ordered a rum and coke. "Why not? This is the Caribbean," he told himself. As he sipped his drink, he wondered if he should look for love again or simply ignore his desire to be with someone. He thought about the single female faculty members he knew. No way, he thought, they were either too bitter or too scientific.

He remembered one who asked him if he would give her a child. She was about to enter menopause and desperate to have children. He was married to April at the time and thought it was a bizarre request coming from a fellow academician. "I should call her when I return. After all, Elsie is not unattractive."

The thought of Elsie's long black hair and dark eyes caused his thoughts to linger as he slowly drank. She had never had time to date while pursuing her doctorate and then later the laborious quest for tenure. Now she appeared desperate. Edmond felt that he would have no difficulty in fulfilling the desires of a woman such as Elsie, but knew that at the present he would not be able to fulfill her immediate needs.

After finishing his drink, he went up to the promenade deck. Instead of the quiet and solitude that he expected, it was filled with joggers. Loud music, escaping from the pool below, motivated the runners to run even faster. He stood to the edge of the jogging track and leaned against the railing. Runners obsessed with the appearance of their bodies sped past him without speaking. His eyes followed the swaying hips of the female joggers but he felt impotent inside.

He turned and looked towards the sea. In the distance, he could see a small interisland freighter. The freighter was headed towards the sinking sun, which meant she was heading west towards the Gulf of Mexico. He remembered the drinks that April and he consumed at the pool bar in Cancun, the sun hot upon their backs, only to be cooled by the ice in their glasses. The clouds, like the surface of the sea, now wore the reflections of early evening.

He thought of the itinerary of the carefully planned trip – the monotony of a tour guide. "Tomorrow we arrive in Barbados. I know little about the island. Perhaps I can catch a flight out to Montserrat, spend a day or two, and return to the ship once she docks in St. Martin. But first I want to take the island tour that my travel agent has already booked. Perhaps it will be more interesting than I think it will be."

Edmond returned to his stateroom and poured himself another drink from a bottle that he had purchased in the ship's store; that drink was soon followed by another.

He sat at the table, preparing his thoughts for writing. He felt unsteady due to the liquor. The room seemed to spin about him. Suddenly he was seated in an elegant dining room. About him were stewards dressed in white and adorned with spotless gloves. His iPad was gone, but in his hand was an ink pen and before him a notebook filled with onionskin paper. He looked at his sleeves. He was dressed in a tuxedo. As he looked about, other guests were dressed formally. The women wore long skirts of fine materials, their hair, depending on age, were covered by exotic hats, many with large feathers adorning them.

At first he panicked, but he forced himself to be calm as his two fellow conversationalists returned to the adjoining table. Punesa wore a striking red dress with multiple strings of pearls about her neck. Her husband's hair was cut shorter now.

As Edmond stared at her, the server appeared in a stiff serving jacket, his hands encased in white gloves. He placed a large menu in Edmond's hands. Before looking at the menu, he noticed the engraving of a ship on the outer binding of the menu and CUNARD LINES in large print. Next to the logo was the pen-and-ink drawing of a large liner.

Then he saw her: Ann Pennington. She appeared like in the photograph on her Facebook page. Her hair was coiffured expertly, exposing the beautiful composition of her face. Her eyes were large and very blue. Even though she wore heels, she appeared to be very small in stature. The eyes, yes, it was the eyes that attracted him. She was with another gentleman when she entered the room. The man appeared to be muscular in build, like a fighter. Neither the man nor the tuxedo complimented the other.

She did not acknowledge Edmond at first. Then she stopped, turned her head and smiled.

Suddenly Edmond was in his own stateroom. He felt ill and possessed a migraine that pounded with each beat of his heart. "What? What? Where am I?" he said out loud. "I was dreaming. What a strange dream. It was too real." Edmond staggered to his feet and fell across his bed, soon asleep again. He did not awaken until he heard noise below his veranda. The ship had arrived in Barbados.

Chapter 4
ESCAPE FROM BARBADOS

Edmond arrived early for breakfast. He was anxious to meet his guide. His travel agent had spent a considerable amount of time looking for just the right person to show him the sights. He was particularly interested in the Redlegs, the remnants of Irish slaves, and the Church of Saint James where his ancestors got married in the 17th century. He often wondered why his forebears had traveled to Barbados to marry on two different occasions and to give birth to his ancestral tree there. It was as far back in time as he could travel in searching for his origins.

The Redlegs were the last remnants of the mythical Irish slaves forced to work in the sugarcane and sea island cotton fields of Barbados. Mythical in the sense that so little was known of them in the years following their captivity. It was, therefore, a race wholly removed from the consciousness of the world.

Edmond looked about the dining room for the couple with whom he had made friends earlier. His eyes searched the darker recesses of the large room. They were not there.

"Good morning, Mario. Have you seen that delightful couple seated across from me last night? I believe their first names are Eric and Punesa. Eric said he was a biologist at a university. I'd like to ask them some more questions about Montserrat. I don't think they ever gave me their last names."

"Oh, you mean the Mayos, Paula and Steven. They were the older couple that sat next to you last night."

"No, I am thinking about the brunette with closely cut bangs. The fellow is a little overweight but nice looking. He too is a brunet. They are young, probably in their mid-twenties. She is very striking. I am sure you remember her."

"Sorry, sir. I believe you are mistaken. The only couple I remember sitting near you were both gray haired, probably in their 60s or early 70s. I remember them clearly since even though guests are not supposed to tip, they left a fifty by their napkin. They were the only people near you that I can remember."

His travel agent had arranged for his tour of Barbados after an Internet search. Only one person, a Pamela Simpson, indicated an interest in being his guide since the request was somewhat unusual. Most tourists only want to know where the beaches are located.

Pamela had given clear instructions on how to find her. "Proceed to the custom's house. I will be waiting under the large tree in front of you."

He was somewhat disappointed when he didn't find her there. Many guides and tourists crowded the small space under the breadfruit tree that provided the only shade for those waiting outside the custom area for a taxi or a tour.

Before long he felt someone touch his shoulder. He turned around and saw a striking woman with light brown skin and large black eyes. Her hair had been straightened and lightly curled about her shoulders.

"Professor Bryant, I assume," said Pamela in a beautiful Creole accent that was melodic in nature.

"Thank you for your willingness to act as my guide," he said as he stared into her eyes. She wore a blue almost military uniform that spoke of her professionalism.

"My pleasure, sir. It is not often that one requests to see the Redlegs. They keep to themselves in a very rural area. Why on earth are you interested in them? Most have lost their teeth, are hemophilic and desperately poor. My father said that ever since Cromwell sentenced them to work the sugarcane and sea island cotton, they resorted to inbreeding as their numbers decreased. I think that there are only about four hundred left of the 40,000 who were sent here. Not one of them ever returned to Ireland. Poor things, they could not afford to after they were freed. Just a forgotten group of people."

She continued, "Everyone, of course, wants to see the Church of Saint James. It is the oldest surviving church on the island. It dates from the latter seventeenth century. Beautiful stone and stained glass. It looks the way a church should look."

Pamela glanced at his luggage, "Here, sir, let me help you with your luggage," she said as he attempted to open the tailgate of her SUV. He noticed the strength of her arms, the supple nature of her moves. "Where would you like to go first?" she asked, shielding her eyes from the bright, unrestrained sun.

He paused. "Let's put off going to the Church of Saint

James for now. I would like to meet at least one disposed Irishman while I am here."

"*Disposed*, yes, that is an interesting choice of words. To dispose of, to get rid of something. That is exactly what Cromwell did to the Irish slaves. Rather than execute them, he thought about how they might yield a profit for the wealthy English of the island."

Edmond looked at her. "I am impressed by your knowledge. You must have studied the subject."

"Yes, I did in preparation for your visit. I am a student at the University of the West Indies and have access to documents, files and books that describe the history of my island. In the 17th century, Cromwell sent over 40,000 Irish slaves to work in the cotton and sugarcane fields. None of them ever returned to Ireland. There are people here that appear to be of Irish descent but are very poor and often diseased. I don't think you will want to see them. Instead, we have many beautiful sites on our island. Let me show you these. Forget the ugly parts. Let me show you our beautiful beaches. I can also point out diving shops. A man like you should stay at Sandals where there is excellent food and yes, beautiful women."

"Pamela, like I said in my e-mail, I want to see the Redlegs or at least attempt to see them. I am looking for someone called Ann Pennington, who may be somehow connected to these people."

"I have never heard of her. I think that you are a very foolish man to pursue such a search. Most of the Redlegs live either on the dry eastern side of our island or in Bridgetown. They run some of the brothels that service middle-class islanders. Your Ann Pennington, if she lives here, may be a madam or a whore."

"Let's not call it a search, let's call it an obsession."

Pamela smiled at him and shook her head.

"Okay, I know that I am a crazy American."

"You must return to your ship by five p.m. or she will sail without you," said Pamela in a serious tone.

"I know. I do not plan on returning to my ship. I can always meet her in another port." He knew that he could not possibly see the historical sites or fulfill his quest to meet the Redlegs with so little time remaining. He also found Pamela an attractive and intelligent person to be with for even a short amount of time.

Pamela drove through the heart of Bridgetown. The tropical trees bent in the trade winds. Red flowers competed with yellow blossoms for his attention. Then the road turned and ran alongside a canal populated with a wide variety of private and commercial boats – island traders, tourist boats and those that belonged to the followers of the sun. People walked without speaking yet seemed to be wearing smiles, perhaps it was the squint caused by the brilliant colors and the reflections of the warm green water.

Pamela turned towards him. "Most of the time, I do not let my guests ride in the front seat, but you seem friendly enough. Some female guides do not like to escort a man alone."

"Well, my friend, it just proves how daring you are. I can assure you that I am harmless. My only viciousness is in my books and they remain unsold. So, you see, you have nothing to fear from me."

"Why do you write if no one reads what you have published? It seems very frustrating and expensive to me."

"You ask a question that I cannot answer. I think it is a compulsion that I have to express myself. You see, I am not a very good conversationalist. I am better with pen and ink than I am in face-to-face encounters."

"Your wife must think otherwise."

"I am sorry, I must not have mentioned in my e-mail that I lost my wife five years ago. I loved her very much. April and I were very close. We had no secrets between us or at least I am certain of that on my part."

Pamela responded, "Suspicion is a prerequisite when it comes to loving someone. Women never tell everything about themselves. Men tend to become jealous too quickly. If a woman has no past, she will find herself of little interest to a man. Men have an innate need to punish themselves."

"I cannot argue with you. You are correct, men are always suspicious. I think it is programmed into our nature. Even on the plains of Africa, you see an innate struggle among the males of all species, at times even deadly in nature," Edmond said as he glanced at Pamela's exposed knees. He quickly looked away towards the Caribbean Sea as she sped along the coast.

"You are a strange man. Why are you seeking this Ann Pennington while you are obviously still in love with your wife? For most men, women are easily forgotten or replaced."

"I don't know how to answer you," Edmond responded. "At times I think April and Ann are the same person."

Pamela looked at Edmond with a serious expression. "I should be more careful when I read e-mails. I suppose I deleted several that I should have kept or failed to read all of them. To be honest, I thought your wife was with you, or I would not have accepted you as a client. A woman always runs a risk when alone even with a man she knows."

"I can assure you I did not mislead you. Why are you so concerned that I came alone?"

"Many bad things can happen to a woman alone in a car with a man."

"I'm sure I mentioned being a professor on sabbatical. Now you don't get any safer than that unless you fear being bored to death."

"What do you want me to call you – Dr. Bryant, Edmond or just Ed?"

"Edmond is fine," he said as he glanced once more at her legs while she shifted gears. He paused. "A manual transmission, that is pretty uncommon these days."

"It gives me more control," she said as she smiled at him.

Pamela pointed with her hand. "Look over there at the unpainted wooden buildings. It is Barbados' red-light district."

Edmond glanced in the direction to which she had pointed. Without bright tropical colors, the brothels stood in stark contrast to the nearby buildings. No customers could be seen walking the street in front of them. It was an area to be avoided when the sun so easily revealed the identity of a potential client.

She glanced at him. "I assume you will need a place to stay since you have jumped ship? May I recommend The Bougainville? It is a fine resort with an excellent beach."

"Don't tell me, your uncle runs it?" Edmond said with a smile.

"No, my younger brother works there. He tends the flowers. He hopes someday to be the manager."

"Yes, I would be interested if you will call and see if they have any vacancies. Is it a safe place?"

"It is one of the safest in the parish. It is gated and has 24-hour security. You will be able to sleep very well there."

They waited at the gate as the security officer checked with the main desk. Then he motioned them through without a smile. The Bougainville was a new resort that combined the traditional with the Caribbean style. It was apparent that her brother was doing a very good job with the flowers for they grew in abundance throughout the well-maintained grounds.

Flowers of every color and variety thrived in the never-ending summer of Barbados. Large broadleaf trees intermixed with palms provided the requisite shade to the individual villas that clustered around the main building that rose five stories above the tropical floor of the gardens.

"When would you like me to pick you up?"

"Give me an hour to get unpacked," he answered.

Without replying, she accelerated down the stone driveway and reentered the busy narrow street that ran in front of The Bougainville. He entered the main lobby where the manager rose to greet him from behind the counter.

"Mr. Bryant, everything is taken care of. I will have the footman take your luggage to your room," said the resort host. "Will you be staying with us long, sir? Your reservation did not indicate the length of your stay."

"How long I stay will depend on what I find out about my distant relative who was married at St. James Church. In addition, I am looking for a friend, a Ms. Ann Pennington. I am hoping to run into her while in Barbados."

"I understand, sir," replied the host who then managed a smile.

Upon entering the room, Edmond opened the shutters that faced a wide private courtyard surrounded by bamboo. In the center of the courtyard was a stone fountain where water splashed in the brilliant light that swept across the paving stones. It was a pleasant place, an oasis of his own.

He positioned his iPad on the desk and adjusted his seat so that it would be at a comfortable writing height. As always, the desk was too high for the desk chair. He took the iPad and placed it on his lap while seated in a dark leather chair. He looked about the room. It was painted in vibrant colors like that of a Matisse painting.

Creative expression did not come to him. His hands remained motionless upon the keyboard. He looked at the glowing empty screen and turned off his iPad. He then positioned his chair so that he could look at the garden and to better hear the splashing of its fountain. The sound of light classical music added to the ambience of the room.

Soon he noticed that it was time to meet Pamela. As he waited in the open-air foyer of the resort, he looked at the tropical colors of the clouds that, like the room, reflected various pastels with varying hues.

Then Pamela approached the stone drive. "Edmond, I hope you like the room that I chose for you."

"It is delightful. You really have good taste."

"Thank you. Now where would you like to go?"

"If it is on the way, let's drive past the brothels that you pointed out earlier. After all, you mentioned that some descendants of the Irish slaves work there. I must admit I am surprised that it is so open here. I remember the red-light district when I was a child in Galveston. I am just as curious now as I was when I was young. Curiosity does not age."

"Do you desire a woman?"

"No." He paused. "Of course, I do. Why lie to you? But this evening I just want to get a feel for Bridgeport and the countryside."

"Do you expect to find Ann Pennington in a brothel?"

"Not really, but nothing in life can surprise me now. The sudden death of my wife and this search for Ann have taken me from the path I had chosen to follow. I guess we cannot be found until we are truly lost."

Pamela drove towards the red-light district of the town. Along the sidewalks, the inhabitants appeared very busy as they talked to one another, staring at passing tourists and hawking a wide variety of vegetables. Pamela drove past the brothels very slowly. Suddenly, Edmond saw an Irish-looking woman at the entrance of a large unpainted building. She stared back at him, her eyes following the slow movement of the car.

"Pamela, I want to return to that brothel tonight," said Edmond.

"Why that one? It's no good. Only cheap sluts work there. Their customers are not even the middle-class men of the city. You are too good for that kind of whorehouse."

As she drove, she pointed towards a small white building where a full-chested Barbadian stood outside. "That's no good either. The women use the playing field across the street to have sex. The men are low class and cannot afford a place to take a woman."

"The playing field? You must be kidding," Edmond said as he looked at the arid field of dirt and dying grass. The few palm trees that outlined the field looked very much out of place.

"Barbadians do not have a lot of money. Some have wives, children and mistresses on whom to spend all their money. My parents were never married. My father now lives with another woman. It is with her that he conceived my brothers and sisters. It was very hard on my mother to support me alone and to send me to college. She loves me very much."

"Does your father not love you also?"

"I don't know. I think that love must be expressed. He only wanted sex with my mother and not a child."

"I am so sorry. Everyone needs to be loved and protected. No matter what gender or age, we all want the Biblical warm wing of a parent," said Edmond.

"I'll take you to the eastern side of the island. Some of the people you seek live there. They are not friendly to outlanders. In fact, they can be aggressive in their unfriendliness."

As they drove, Edmond saw for the first time the sugarcane and sea island cotton that had brought so much misery to the Irish slaves. On the hills appeared stone structures much like Roman watchtowers. "Pamela, what are those buildings?"

"They are the foundations of the windmills that were once used in the sugar-extracting process. There is only one left capable of fulfilling its original function, and it is for tourists. Are you hungry?"

"Yes, indeed I am, but I don't see any restaurants in the area."

"No problem, my almost boyfriend has a café nearby where he serves the island specialty – flying fish," said Pamela, smiling.

"Seriously, *flying fish?* I thought they were considered trash fish. When I was in the Navy, I remember the bow of my destroyer harvesting them."

"Flying fish are very good to eat. They are our national fish. Hunger, special seasoning, sea salt and deep-fat frying make any fish good, even trash fish."

They entered the small open-air café that was aptly named The Flying Fish. "The owner wants to date me. I have told him no over and over. He is too old and serious for me. I want a good-looking young man who will support me. My last boyfriend, he lived with me for two years. He got mad when I refused to cook for him. He left."

"I am sorry," replied Edmond.

"My first boyfriend lived in my house. He refused to move out when I broke up with him. My father wanted to kill him. Instead, I burned the house down to get rid of him."

"I assume he was not in the house when you burned it?" asked Edmond.

"Unfortunately, he wasn't," Pamela replied.

"I can certainly appreciate why you've raised your standards when it comes to gentlemen friends."

The owner came to the table and proceeded to take the order. He stared for a minute at Pamela, who did not acknowledge him, then left after they had ordered to cook the flying fish. The sound of boiling grease could be heard as the fish were lowered into the cauldron nourished by butane.

"I am sorry for him, but I do not find him attractive. He just wants to be a lover. He is just like my father, he just wants sex."

Edmond spoke as he fanned a hungry insect away from the just served fish. "I was really surprised when I saw the sea island cotton. The stalks are more like hedges than the cotton that I am used to seeing. I also noticed that the sugarcane is very short and unattended."

"The soil is worn out, and it has been very dry. The sugar industry in Barbados is dying since no one wants to work in the sun. When the slaves first arrived, the land was fertile. There were rain forests then."

"You mean you don't have rain forests anymore? I thought that most of the Caribbean islands had at least a small one."

"We do have a remnant of the rain forest. It surrounds a very old Episcopal church. The forest is now protected but it is only a portion of what it used to be."

"I would like to see it if you don't mind."

"Of course, it is near here. As soon as we finish our fish, we can go."

The weather in Barbados does not change dramatically. The trade winds keep the island free of oppressive heat and humidity. The land, however, being stripped of its native vegetation. appeared hot and arid.

As they drove, Pamela pointed towards some animals grazing on a small hillock. "Look over there. You will see our Blackbelly sheep."

"Where?" asked Edmond. "All I see are goats."

Pamela laughed. "They are not goats, they are sheep. Look at their tails. If they stand up, they are sheep; if their tails lie down, they are goats. Blackbelly sheep only live on this island. A sheep with thick wool could not survive."

"What value are sheep with no wool?" asked Edmond.

"We eat them. Their meat is too expensive for most people. They are mainly served to the tourists. Some locals will eat them, but it is only for a special occasion."

"I wish people could adapt that quickly to the heat and sun. It must have been terrible for the Irish who were stripped of their clothing, religion and culture. I am surprised that any of them have survived."

"Before I show you the rain forest, I want to take you to the coast where the Atlantic Ocean smacks the island. There is a man from Portugal who owns a bar and a restaurant there. There is also a cave, but he charges admission if you want to enter it."

It was but a short drive to the open-air bar. Before it the deep blue and turbulent Atlantic pounded upon the coral reefs and ancient volcanic rock of the island. The rocks appeared to be soft, beaten by storms for centuries. The waves rose and crashed upon the cliff below them. The beauty of the scenery undisturbed by those that inhabit the island.

After ordering some rum punch, they sat silently looking

at the sea. For the first time, he noticed Pamela's natural beauty, her long legs and ample breasts. Her flawless skin retained the glow of youth while her optimism buoyed his sprit. It was as though she were a model Paul Gauguin had painted while visiting the Caribbean prior to his journeys to the South Seas.

Edmond imagined her as the subject for a painting. He visualized red flowers in her hair while she lay on a beach of white sand. He spoke above the sounds of the sea. "Have you ever dated one of your clients?"

"No… well, maybe you could call it a date. A very old professor came to the island to do research. He hired me to be his companion for the week. He was interested in the wild orchids that only grow in the rain forest of Barbados. The professor wanted to record information about them before they were lost due to the changing climate and pollution generated by the island. He was alone like you. His wife had also died many years before. The professor said he never would marry again. He had basked deeply in the perfection of their love and could not love that way again."

"Are those his words or yours?"

"His. I do not think like he does. For me there is always a future, and a man is going to be a part of it."

"You said a date – it sounds more like a care service for an elderly scholar."

"You should not say that. Someday you will be that professor. When does a man or a woman stop needing love? Do we ever not want to be touched or held? Age does not affect our need for another."

He responded, "Desire in old age quickly turns to need."

Edmond wanted very much to place the palm of his hand

on her resting hand but hesitated. She could only be viewed as a friend since they had just met. Edmond realized how weak he was at that moment. He was too vulnerable in Pamela's presence, too alone emotionally to be rational.

The rum punch tasted very good. The cold liquid made him feel relaxed almost to the point of recklessness. The wind grew stronger as clouds from the Atlantic raced over the island towards the Caribbean Sea.

Pamela and Edmond left the bar and drove along the winding coastal road. Small structures appeared in the water like manmade stone buildings.

"What are those?" Edmond asked.

"They are our famous standing stones. The sea cuts at the base creating a pedestal upon which the majority of the remaining stone perches. See, someone has built a small dwelling atop one of them."

Edmond felt amazed. In his travels, he had never seen such rock formations on a beach.

The road took them back to the highlands and then to the cotton and sugarcane fields. Suddenly, Pamela swerved into a narrower road. Large trees began to appear while gentle rain fell on the windshield. Just off the road was a small Episcopal church, its stone walls darkened by the rains of centuries. In the grounds of the church were the remnants of a rain forest. As they drove further, the clouds darkened and rain fell heavily. Monkeys appeared at the edge of the road. As they drove past, Edmond saw a red-haired woman with a large python around her shoulders.

"Pamela, stop! There is a woman there that I want to meet. Back up!" he shouted.

Pamela immediately stopped the car and put it in reverse. Her backing was erratic, swerving from one side of the road to the other. When they reached the point where the woman had been standing, Pamela stopped. "Edmond, there is no one here. If she was where you thought that she was, she probably left due to the rain."

"I tell you, she was here. Right at the base of that large tree," said Edmond as he pointed towards the towering tree. "She had a python around her shoulders!"

Pamela laughed. "I think you have drunk too many rum punches. You only thought you saw someone. My psychology teacher taught me that we see what we want to see. We all have selective vision. You wanted to see Ann so you saw her, but only you. Besides, the rain distorts what we see."

Rain continued to streak down the windows of the car as Edmond said, "Pamela, perhaps you are right. There is no one here. You did see the monkeys, didn't you?"

"Yes, I did. They live here, you know."

"When we return to Bridgetown, I would like to visit the red-light district tonight. I want to visit a brothel where the women are light in color, perhaps descendants of the Irish. Do you know of such a brothel?" he asked hesitantly.

"Yes, I think I do. It is called The King's Head."

"That is a strange name for a brothel."

"What you ask for is strange. Do you only want to be with a white woman?"

"No, I didn't say that. I want to talk to some of the prostitutes."

"What about?"

"Maybe I can learn more about the Redlegs from them.

After all, you did mention that a few of them became prostitutes. Perhaps one of the sex workers has heard of Ann Pennington."

That evening Pamela returned at nine. Edmond was waiting inside the main building entrance for her. As she drove into the gateway, he put out his cigarette and placed his piña colada on the bannister of the lobby.

She looked at his wide-brimmed straw hat and loose white cotton shirt and pants. "Trying to fit in?" she said with a laugh.

"Is it that obvious? Yes, I am attempting to get into character, I am trying to look like a stereotypical expat," Edmond said, smiling. Their eyes met for a brief moment.

"I sure hope you know what you are doing. You know that the King's Head caters to middle-class and wealthy black men. I don't care what you wear, you will be totally out of your comfort zone."

"Thanks for the warning. I am sure I need it. If I am going to find Ann, I have to take chances."

"Taking chances for a person that does not exist? By the way, do you have enough money? They have a thing about people paying their bills upfront. I would not use a credit card there. If you do, you might as well put your card number on the Internet."

"Don't worry, I will be careful not to spend all of my money at the King's Head."

"Spoken like a wise fool!" She laughed. She knew that when faced with temptation, men always yielded. More so if that temptation is a beautiful young woman who has mastered the art of seduction. Eyes are the passport to a man's wealth and his soul.

The King's Head was just off Canal Street in a less prosperous section of Bridgetown, sandwiched between a popular resort and the poorest area of the city. As they approached, he could see the deteriorating exterior of the building. Light escaped through the cracks in the front door, which was partially ajar. Dim lights could be seen on the second story where a woman leaned out from a casement window and peered down at Edmond as the car stopped.

"When do you want me to pick you up? I don't think you can afford an overnight stay," she said in a manner that denoted a degree of caution.

"I will call you on my cell phone. I have no idea how long this will take," Edmond said as he opened his car door. Pamela then accelerated her car into the dark street. As he approached the building, he could feel people staring at him even though he could not yet see them. He slowly walked up the three wooden steps and pushed the door open. Celtic music could be heard. It was an old Enya CD from the 1990s, hauntingly beautiful.

No one approached him as he looked into a bar that also served as the foyer. A young Irish-looking woman stood behind the bar, still and silent like a mime. A large Barbadian stood at the end of the bar and glared at the intruder.

A heavyset woman approached him. "Are you British?" she asked. "If you are, get the hell out!"

"No, I am not. I am a traveler."

"What do you want, unknown man?" asked the bouncer.

"I want to buy some time."

The madam replied, "That will cost you more than a lay."

"I know, but time is what I am seeking."

"It will cost you five hundred dollars to sit at the bar and watch. Are you a voyeur? If so, I can accommodate you more cheaply in one of our rooms upstairs."

"No, I don't want to watch someone have sex. I would like to talk to you and to the women who work here."

"Listen, Unknown, talking is something we don't do."

"Okay, how about five hundred and a hundred for each woman that talks to me?" Edmond replied.

"Let me see your cash," the madam demanded.

"I have a thousand in my wallet." He opened his wallet and placed ten one-hundred dollar bills on the table.

"Before we agree to your demand, I need to be sure this is not entrapment. Are you in any way connected to law enforcement here in Barbados or anywhere else in the world?"

"No, I am not connected to any law enforcement agency," Edmond replied.

"So, you are just a sick pervert who wants to pleasure himself while he talks to women? I see you have an iPad with you, do you want to take pictures of the girls? That is forbidden at the King's Head."

"No, I am just a faculty member who needs to complete his doctor of sociology degree in order to get tenure at my university. I have chosen as my doctoral dissertation topic, 'The History of the Irish Slave in the Caribbean.' I am hoping that you or some of your sex workers are descendants of the Redlegs. If so, I need to jot down some notes. I hope that explains why I have an iPad with me."

The madam replied, "I don't know who or what my ancestors were. Some cursed bastards I would say. That is probably true of the rest of the girls here. 'Sex worker' – I like that term. Most of us refer to ourselves as hookers. Our clients call us whores, but you scholars have such nice terms to describe everything."

One by one, Edmond interviewed the women in the brothel, just quick questions to determine who if any considered themselves to be Redlegs. The last person interviewed seemed interested in his questions. She had natural red hair and possessed a freshness that the other women had lost. She seemed innocent yet was guilty of practicing the oldest of illegal professions.

"What is your name?" asked Edmond.

"Magdalene," she replied, staring into his eyes.

"That is a pretty name. I assume you consider yourself to be Irish with such a name."

"Yes, I do," she replied as she lit a cigarette.

"Good, then I have several questions I would like to ask you."

"First, you must pay me and order me a shot of Jameson," she said without the warmth of a smile. It was apparent that she was a professional void of any emotion.

"Of course," he said as he placed a new bill in her hand and ordered the drink from the madam. "Did you know your father and mother?"

"Yes," she replied.

"Where did they come from?"

"Barbados."

"I see, they were born here. What about your grandparents?"

"I don't have any."

"We all have grandparents."

"I don't know anything about them."

"Do you have brothers and sisters?"

"Yes, but I do not know them. They live on the other side of the island. I have not seen them since I left home."

"How can you not know them when you all live on such a small island?" asked Edmond.

"They stayed on the land where I was born while I went to Bridgetown. We have nothing in common, so we never see one another."

"Have you ever known anyone named Ann?"

"White or black?"

"White, a girl just like you with red hair and blue eyes. Perhaps a little smaller than you."

"How old is she?"

"I don't know," Edmond replied.

"Why do you ask me questions about a girl you don't even know?"

"I am trying to find her."

"I thought you were interested in the Redlegs and their history. It sounds to me like you are trying to find someone in particular."

"I don't know if you can understand what I am going to say next. You see I don't know if she is still alive or even if she exists."

"Are you on drugs?" Magdalene asked in a serious tone.

"No, but please tell me – do you know anyone with that

name?"

"Yes, the madam took several of her girls to Montserrat. I don't really know why she chose that island. None of us had ever been there and two of the girls had never even heard of it. All I knew was that a volcano exploded and destroyed the capital city in the 1950s. The British government does not want anyone to return to the island since the volcano is still active."

"An island named Montserrat and it is British?"

"Yes, it is a protectorate of Britain," Magdalene replied.

"What is the connection between Ann and the island?" Edmond asked.

"Well, one day I was walking down a path to the beach. I heard a girl crying. There on the beach was a woman who looked a lot like me. She was kneeling on the sand. In her hand was a rosary.

"I asked her what was wrong. She only looked at me. Then I asked her what her name was. She did not reply. She took a small piece of driftwood and wrote her name on the sand. I tried to get her to tell me more about herself but she would not. I think that some Redlegs might have been resettled on Montserrat after slavery ended. Perhaps she was one of the daughters of our cursed race."

"Tell me more about this Ann. What was she wearing?"

"A green shift I think. She did not have a hat on which means she was about to get really sunburned."

"I can't imagine anyone with Irish blood not wearing a hat on a tropical beach," replied Edmond.

Magdalene paused. "Why are you really here? To hear about a girl that you do not know, or to have sex with me, a woman that is real?"

"That is a probing and blunt question," said Edmond.

"You already paid me for my time. It doesn't matter if you just want to talk or have sex," she said, staring into his eyes. "What if I told you I was Ann? Would you spend more money on me?"

"I don't know how to respond to your question. I suppose I would."

"From now on, I will tell any man who asks that my name is Ann," she said, laughing. "I will tell you more about your Ann if you take me upstairs."

The music of the bar increased in volume as did the alcoholic content of his drinks. His will to resist her request vanished. She took his hand and led him to the steep wooden stairs that led to the rooms above. Edmond felt light-headed as though he were entering a dream state. She walked ahead of him, holding his hand. As they entered the second-story hallway, Edmond noticed how quiet the rooms were. There were no sounds being emitted. Even their footsteps were muted.

Edmond entered her room. There was a large unmade bed and a small dresser. On her dresser was a single rose, now wilting in the heat of the room. The single bathroom at the end of the hallway served the needs of the second floor.

"Before we make love, please drink this. It will make you a better lover," she said quietly.

Edmond took the glass from her hand and drank it. He quickly felt weak as though he had developed hypoglycemia. He eased himself into the only chair in the small room and lost any awareness of his surroundings and of Magdalene.

In his dream, he was walking in the shallow surf, his feet feeling the sand and the warm waters of the Caribbean Sea.

Then he saw Ann kneeling alone. As he approached her, she did not respond or turn her head towards him. Instead, she fell over on her side and broke into glass shards that were soon lost in the churning of the black sand.

Edmond felt the pain first in his head. He tried to open his eyes wide but one eye was swollen completely shut. He raised himself to a sitting position. He looked around only to see stalks of sugarcane around him. He fell backwards on the ground and passed out again.

He awoke as a renewed sense of pain reached his consciousness. He rested his pounding head on his knees. He slowly raised himself up even though he was unsteady at first. He touched his pants' pocket to make sure his wallet was still there. To his amazement, it was. He knelt once more on the ground hoping to find his iPad but could not locate it in the dense sugarcane. He thought how fortunate that he had locked his passport in the room's safe. Also in the safe was the remainder of the money he had saved for the trip.

Other than the rising moon that sat just above a distant ridge, the night was very dark. From far away, he could hear a dog barking. He stumbled to the edge of the road and then fell to his knees. He raised himself to an upright position as he waited to hail any vehicle that passed by.

After a long wait, he saw the lights of a truck approaching him. Edmond realized that he was covered in blood from superficial abrasions that covered his face and hands. The open wound on the back of his head still oozed hot, sticky blood. He realized that his appearance might forestall anyone from stopping to render aid.

In the distance, he could still see the headlights of the vehicle winding through the rain forest. A sense of renewed fear gripped him. The truck was traveling very quickly towards him.

He crawled back into the small rock drainage ditch and began to move rapidly as he reentered the sugarcane. Just as he feared, the vehicle stopped where he had earlier emerged from the growth. Immediately, the lights of the truck were cut off. Two large men, a Latin American and a Barbadian judging from their accents, quickly got out of the car. They looked both ways and rapidly entered the sugarcane field, pointing the beams of their flashlights in all directions as they searched for him.

He could hear them talking but could not make out any of the words spoken, only their accents. Soon they emerged from the field and reentered the parked vehicle where a third man waited. Then they drove a short distance, stopped, argued and then drove away until Edmond could no longer see their headlights.

After waiting a short time, he walked towards a small house where the barking dogs soon awakened the owner who quickly emerged onto the porch with a cutlass.

"Sir, I have been injured. I need your help," said Edmond, still dazed.

"What you say?"

"I said I need help and have been injured." He could tell that the man on the porch still could not understand him. Instead he grasped the hilt of his cutlass tighter. He pointed the blade towards Edmond.

Edmond spoke louder. "I don't have a car. Would you call my friend to pick me up? I will pay you for your trouble."

Edmond wondered why they had left his wallet with the cash still inside it. It was obvious that they had planned on taking him somewhere else where they could leave him after staging an accident. Otherwise they would have killed him in the sugarcane field.

After receiving a call, Pamela drove towards him even though it was close to three in the morning before she arrived. His head continued to bleed while the pain increased.

She saw Edmond standing in the middle of the road. "You said you were injured. What on earth happened to you?"

"It seems like I must have offended someone at the King's Head."

"Not too difficult to do considering what they are and their clientele. People who go there want to keep it hush-hush. If they have a problem, they will not call the police or complain. Prostitution and drugs are illegal on our island. This is especially true for foreigners."

As she opened the car door to help him in, she noticed his head wound. "I'll tie a scarf around your head. Maybe that will stop the bleeding. I don't want all that blood on my car seat. After all, this vehicle is rented."

"Rented?" asked Edmond.

"Yes, rented. Do you think I can afford such a nice vehicle on what I make?"

Edmond did not reply. He struggled to remain conscious as she drove to The Bougainville. Almost immediately, he passed out again. It was still dark when he awoke. The bleeding had stopped and the pain was now tolerable.

After regaining consciousness, Edmond opened the door to his villa. Inside his room, one of the lamps was glowing. Seated in a wingback chair was Magdalene.

"You are lucky to be alive," she said. "When I heard someone on the veranda, I saw you being helped by a woman. I went outside to assist her. You looked like you had been badly injured. We helped you to a porch chair and then she left."

"What on earth are you doing here?" asked Edmond. "Why did you leave me on the porch? Why didn't you help me inside?"

"I tried to but you just wanted to stay seated, and then you were not awake. You were too heavy for me to carry."

"But why are you here?" questioned Edmond.

"I came back to your room to escape being killed. When you asked about Ann Pennington and they saw your military ID, they thought the two of you must be working together. You see, Ann's body was found in the harbor. She was fully clothed, even money was in her pocket. They suspected she was working for some foreign government. Since I'm the last to talk to you about Ann, they think I must be working with you. That is why we must leave Barbados immediately."

"Why don't you leave with me for the States? We can catch an early flight."

"I am not a citizen of your country and cannot leave. In fact, I am not even a citizen of Barbados. Many of us exist as shadow people. Will you take me to the island of Montserrat? They will not look for me there. There are others on the island that are descendants of the Irish. I can blend into the island's population. I think that Ann's family may still be there. If so, they will protect us."

"Do Ann's parents know she was murdered?"

"Yes, they must know. They will want nothing more than vengeance. You know, the Irish do not forget or forgive. This is especially true if a daughter is murdered."

"You want me to take you to an island I had not heard of except when a couple mentioned it on the cruise ship? I must admit I planned on going there myself. All right, since I got you into this situation, how do we get to the island?"

"They will think you will attempt to fly to safety. Once they see you at the airport, they will either kill you there or wait for you to land. They have many friends in foreign countries. Since they have seen your ID, they now know your name and where you live. You will never be safe just as I will never be. No government can protect you."

"I will have to think about what you just said." He paused. "You still haven't answered my question – how are we going to get off this island?"

"I have a relative that has a small sailboat. Before I returned to your room, I called him. My uncle owes me money and a favor. He told me tonight that we can take his boat. In fact, he mentioned that if I needed to, I could keep the boat."

"I must know something. Why are they willing to kill anyone? What did Ann know?"

"I do not really know. I know they are dangerous. I am certain they killed Ann. She was afraid of water. She never would have gone on a boat yet she was found drowned. The authorities, however, only assumed that it was Ann based on her clothing. The sea and the fish had rendered her visually unidentifiable. The government will not investigate further. In their way of thinking, she was only a shadow person. Can you sail a small boat?" Magdalene asked.

"Yes, I assume it is a sloop?"

"I think so. It has two small sails. The boat is docked at my uncle's pier that he built. He is too lazy to stow the sails below deck. He just wraps them around the boom and mast."

Edmond realized he was being swept into circumstances that he had no control over. His life had always been one of conformity. But ever since April's death, it seemed to have become one of confusion. He felt that he no longer made decisions but only reacted to events around him.

"Why not go to the police?" he asked himself. "No, I can't do that. I was in a brothel when all this started. They would just take a report, and then I would be on my own without any police protection. Magdalene is right, perhaps this is my only chance to survive until I can think everything through more clearly."

Edmond's head ached and his vision was very blurry in one eye. They had hoped to find the vessel tied to her uncle's small pier, instead the sailboat was moored to a buoy just off the beach. They waded as far as they could, then swam the short remaining distance to the vessel. Luckily, there was a boarding ladder swung over the side that allowed them to crawl aboard. The salt water burned the deep wound on the back of his head.

In the dark, Edmond entered the small, cramped cabin that contained two seaman's berths and also housed the small Atomic 4 engine that dated from the 1960s. He knew something about this type of gasoline engine since his father had owned a similar one when the family lived near Lake Guntersville. Edmond touched the starter and the engine came alive. He placed the shift bar into the gear slot and pulled back the lever. The boat moved forward, its low-torque engine turning an oversized propeller blade.

Having taken the slack off the mooring chain, Edmond put the engine in neutral and moved forward to release the sailboat. Soon they were clear of the small bay. The trade wind provided a constant source of energy as they raised the main and the jib. Because of the strength of the wind, Edmond soon lowered the jib, leaving only the mainsail to gather the trapped wind. They quickly reefed it when they came close to capsizing. The trip to Montserrat began in a rising sea.

"Magdalene, from the chart in the cabin, it shows that we are 302 miles from Montserrat. If we have a problem, we can stop at St. Lucia, Dominica or Guadeloupe for repairs or assistance. We are fortunate that there are so many islands to choose from."

Magdalene replied, "Let's pray that we make it. If we stop at another island, there may be questions asked that we cannot answer. In a sense, we could become the fugitives. I do not know what will happen to us if we are sent back to Barbados."

Fortunately, the trade winds provided the force and needed direction to take them on a close-hauled course towards the island. The waves, sliced by the sharp bow, cast water upon the decks and the boat's crew. The small well-built native craft quickly found her stride in the winds.

The sun was just coming up over the swells. From the locker, they found additional charts. Since Edmond had served as a naval officer, he was familiar with charts and navigation. He could, however, only estimate their position since he did not have a sextant or a GPS to aid them. There was no way he could account for the set and drift of the vessel. He knew, however, that by sighting various islands, he could obtain a rough estimate of their location.

Magdalene was silent as the boat rose and fell into the troughs of the swells. The air smelled of salt, the morning clouds wore the colors of sunrise. Earlier, gulls had been their companions, now only a lone albatross rode the wind with them. Being early June, there were no threats of hurricanes, only clouds to give them occasional shade.

Magdalene's red hair captured the color of the rising sun. Her eyes were a Caribbean Sea color and her skin fair. She was still wearing the short floral-print dress she had on in the brothel. He noticed she did not have any shoes or a hat to keep the sun from blistering her.

"I see you have not brought anything with you. Luckily for us, your uncle provided the boat with water and some fruit to eat."

Edmond continued, "Judging from the boat itself, your uncle must have fished for a living. It is a solid, heavily-built boat. Unfortunately, she is also slow. But unless the pursuers figure out the connection between your uncle, the boat and us, we should be safe for the moment. We look just like any other local boat in these waters."

"Yes, my uncle does some fishing. Of course, he has to have other jobs in order for his family to survive. He also works in the cotton and sugarcane fields. He fishes so that his family has something to eat and he sells the rest of the fish in the market or to a local café. Flying fish always bring good money since they are our national symbol and taste very good when fried."

"I can certainly attest to that." He paused. "You are not a citizen of Barbados yet you just said *our* national symbol."

"I was born in a wooden house built by my father. He never had anything except what he could grow or gather with his hands. The country of Barbados had no interest in us."

"I am sorry. One thing I must say is that you are definitely of Irish ancestry with your bright red hair and very blue eyes."

"Yes, I descended from Irish slaves. For over three hundred years, we have suffered from what Cromwell did to us. We have no religion, songs or history. We are people without our own souls."

Edmond stared at her. For the first time, he noticed her as a woman. Young, beautiful and, in her own way, innocent. "I like to think that every morning we begin again, just as the day does. Visitors in a lovely garden."

"You must be religious. I really don't know what religion is about."

"Well, first, you have to trust someone you love. If that is not possible, then you cannot love a God that is not seen but only felt within us. There was a time when I was religious, but that was long ago and in another land."

After several hours, an island with clouds entangled among its peaks appeared off to port. "If I am correct, that should be Saint Lucia. We will be able to tell from the Pitons." Soon the vessel passed the two well-known mountains off her beam. "The next island will be Martinique. From then on, we will see one island after another. We are really fortunate there are so many islands close by in case the weather turns foul. This time of year squalls usually appear in the afternoon and then quickly disappear. There should not be any bad storms, but the ocean is filled with uncertainties."

Edmond found two warm beers and several dried fish in the locker. "This is not exactly my idea of eating out, but at least we have something to nourish us. Since I am going to an island I know nothing about, can you tell me why there are Irish descendants there?"

"I suppose they were slaves just like we were in Barbados."

"I seem to have read somewhere a long time ago that they were resettled there once white slavery ended in the 1800s. I may, of course, be mistaken."

"Edmond, regardless of why they are there, the island is known by two names: The Emerald Island and the Pompeii of the Caribbean. It has two spirits."

"I hope we are not going to Montserrat simply because some promoter refers to it as 'Emerald Island.'"

"No, Ann talked about it. It seems like she lived there at one time. If I remember correctly, she was born there. It is true that most of the people are biracial, only a very few are like Ann."

"If we make it safely to Montserrat, what will you do?" asked Edmond.

"What I have always done," she said quietly to herself.

They looked away. Then, at first softly, Magdalene began to sing. Her voice was clear and beautiful. To him, it seemed like God's gift to one of his weakest of children. She sang "The Emigrants Story," a beautiful haunting story of a person leaving their love behind as they traveled across the seas to America. Edmond had heard it sung before in Dublin's Temple Bar district.

"Your voice is beautiful. Truly beautiful. Why don't you sing instead of working in a brothel? You are wasting your God-given talent."

She looked at him through her wind-tossed hair. "Who would hire me? There is no demand for an Irish girl to sing such songs in Bridgetown. Men come there to get drunk and get laid. That is all they want."

"Magdalene, surely there is somewhere where your talents would be appreciated. If I remember correctly, there was once a recording studio in Montserrat. It seems like the producer of the Beatles set up a studio there. I think several artists went to Montserrat for a recording since they found the beauty and serenity of the island very conducive to creativity."

"That was before the Soufrière Hills volcano erupted and Hurricane Hugo destroyed what remained. Now there is nothing on the island except a few bars and restaurants. Tourists do not come there since the commercial dock in Plymouth was destroyed. There is no pier-side mooring for cruise ships. Even if there were, the island remains too dangerous. The last eruption was in 1997 and she still smolders, waiting, just waiting."

"How do you know all of this?" asked Edmond.

"Ann loved to talk about her home. She must have been very happy there. Because of the volcano, the beaches are black yet truly beautiful in their uniqueness. I understand that there are crystals of green and red that blend in with the black sand.

They say if the sun is just right, the colors mix and sparkle. Of course, it could just be a promotional gimmick to boost tourism."

Magdalene continued, "Ann spoke of a beach there that is truly amazing. It has black sand and faces the sea cliffs."

"What will we do with the boat when we arrive?" asked Edmond.

"I guess we can sell it, but I think it would be safer if we sank it. If no one sees it, then no questions would be raised. My uncle said it was okay to get rid of it. When he asked where we were going, I told him it was best that he not know. He was kind enough to stock the boat with what he had and to give us the charts of all the islands and a compass. He also gave us some foul weather gear to prevent too much exposure to the sea and sky."

"I wondered why this boat was so well stocked. You owe him a lot for what he did," said Edmond.

"Someday I will repay him," she said as she wiped away a tear.

The hours of their first day at sea passed quickly. While he was confident that it was possible to reach Montserrat in two days, he could not be certain. Just before sunset, a flying fish leaped onto the bow of the boat. Magdalene swiftly grabbed it and handed the fish to Edmond who gutted it. The small alcohol stove was lit and soon the fish was frying in the pan.

"Look what I found hidden beneath some lines – a bottle of Barbados rum. It is not one of the fancy types you can buy in hotels. It was bootlegged by my uncle. He uses the same sugarcane that finer rums use, plus some of his own improvisations. It makes it even sweeter," said Magdalene.

Edmond looked at the bottle. "Are you sure it is safe to drink? It smells like a mixture of liquor and gasoline."

Magdalene laughed. "Of course, it is. If the Atomic 4 can run on it, we can too."

"I assume that information on engine fuel is on the label." Edmond smiled.

They soon became very hungry as the smell of frying fish filled the air. They knew there would not be much to eat from so small a fish, but they thrived on anticipation.

"What do we have to go with it?" asked Edmond.

"I found some bananas and coconuts in the galley," Magdalene replied.

"Galley, you mean that wash tub stowed away forward?"

"Yes, any sailor knows that coconuts can sustain you with their liquid and meat. They also do not spoil, so many sailors store them onboard just in case."

"I assume this is a 'just in case' moment."

Soon the national fish of Barbados was shared on a small metal plate. They made sure that the other had at least a taste of the delicate white meat. Edmond gave the larger portion to Magdalene whose small frail body desperately needed nourishing.

As the sun touched the swells of the sea, they both listened for the legendary sizzle as it burned the waves.

"Here," Magdalene said as she handed Edmond a sextant and the necessary manuals to establish their position. "I found them under a loose board forward of the galley. My uncle must have hidden them there since they are of great value to any sailor. Now you will not have to guess our position."

"I haven't use a sextant since I was in the Navy. This is a nostalgic moment for me," Edmond said with a laugh. "Let's hope I can still remember how to figure out our latitude and longitude."

The evening star glistened in the western sky. Nearby was another star almost equal to it in brilliance. Magdalene looked at him as he pointed the instrument first towards Mercury and then Venus. "How do you know they are planets and not stars?" she asked.

"If they do not flicker, they are planets. Besides, look how bright they are, especially Venus."

Soon he finished his calculations. "Martinique is just to the west of us." They looked towards the distant island, the summits of its hills and jagged highlands crowned with low clouds. "If you had not suggested Montserrat, I would have chosen that island," he said, pointing towards Martinique.

"Why?" asked Magdalene.

"Ernest Hemingway wrote a story during World War II. The actual setting was Cuba, but President Franklin Delano Roosevelt did not want to anger the Hispanic world, so he persuaded Ernest and his writing assistant, William Faulkner, to change the location of the book to Martinique."

"Well? That doesn't exactly answer my question," she responded.

"To be honest, the attraction to me was that the movie starred Humphrey Bogart and Lauren Bacall. I think it was her first movie. They fell in love on the set; real chemistry between those two. I have to admit that when Lauren did a dance towards the end of the movie, she became the most sensual woman I have ever seen."

"That is why you would have gone to Martinique? Did the movie show what the island actually looked like?"

"No, of course not, it was shot on a set. It was World War II, and there were German U-boats in the area," Edmond said with a smile.

"So you really don't know anything about the island. You probably do not know that it is French. Don't you know what the French think of the Irish?"

"Okay, so I would have gotten us in trouble."

"You could have put us in harm's way had we gone there. The owner of the King's Head has friends there. It is best to stay seaward of the island."

The wind began to die. The sounds of the boat became louder as the sea abated. The flapping of the sails, the squeaking of the hull and the lapping of the water against the hull produced the unique sounds common to any sailing vessel that is becalmed.

"I can tell that you were married at one time. Are you still married or are you divorced?" Magdalene asked.

"Widowed, I fear."

"What was her name?" Magdalene inquired.

"April."

"Since we have many hours remaining in the voyage, please tell me about her. I am always curious why a man chooses to love a woman. It is obvious that your relationship was not built on sex alone. You haven't even made a pass at me."

"It is too painful for me to discuss with you."

"I understand," she said tenderly.

Edmond looked at the dark sea upon whose swells the moon sailed. The sea awakened thoughts that he had suppressed until now, memories that haunted both his dreams and waking moments.

After a fitful sleep, Edmond awoke to the morning light. He had not intended to sleep on the watch. While there was not a lot of ocean-going traffic in their vicinity, there was enough to cause potential problems. Based on his own experiences at sea, even a distant speck on the horizon can eventually result in a collision.

He did not think that the Barbadians would trace them quickly. There was nothing remarkable about the boat except for the very long bowsprit that added not only to her length but to her speed. The beautiful traditional lines of the vessel might draw attention in any port they entered.

Around 10:00, a small seaplane approached them from just above the horizon. Magdalene rose to an upright position. "Could they have found us this quickly? Even if they tortured him, my uncle could not tell them where we are heading."

"No, that would be impossible. It must be someone just flying for fun who spotted us. Sailboats make beautiful photographs, especially those that are locally built," said Edmond confidently.

The small aircraft glistened in the tropical sun as it approached them. As the engine sound became increasingly audible, Magdalene hid herself under a tarpaulin. It made a pass around them and then another. Edmond waved at the plane, pretending to be a fisherman since it was apparent that their boat was locally built.

The plane rocked its wings in response. He could not tell if the aircraft was private or belonged to a local government. Edmond knew that there was ongoing concern with drug traffickers using local craft so as not to garner suspicion.

When the aircraft could no longer be heard, Magdalene emerged from under the tarpaulin. "I realize I should not be so concerned, but anything out of the ordinary scares me. I know that whoever killed Ann must have a powerful reach and will stop at nothing to kill us."

"Magdalene, you overestimate our importance. They are probably content that we have vanished. They know we cannot go to the authorities on any island," said Edmond as he scanned the sky and sea.

"You are wrong. I overheard their plan to dispose of her body. I am the only one, aside from you, that can testify against them."

"You forget one thing – if they are as well funded and organized as you believe them to be, they have influence with the local government and police. They will, in most likelihood, be immune from any prosecution," said Edmond.

"They are but a tentacle of the octopus. The octopus will never tolerate attention being brought to itself. They intend for us to vanish without a trace. They will not stop searching until we are dead."

The sun burned their fair skin. The one item that they so desperately needed – sunscreen – was not in the boat's inventory. The wind was dying as the vessel rode the large swells that were no longer driven by the wind. The boom squeaked loudly as it rocked back and forth carrying the weight of the limp main sail. The jib had lost its form and lay dormant before them.

Soon they spotted a small craft heading their way. They could see the roster tail formed by its wake. It was obviously a cigarette boat with tremendous horsepower, the type that drug runners use. As it neared and commenced to circle, they could see it was painted black. No flag was flying from the sternpost.

Magdalene once more sought the shelter of the tarpaulin. Edmond reached for the fishing gear making a cast in the direction of the approaching boat. The boat slowed as it neared them. It rose on the wake it had created. With its engine running quietly, no one appeared on deck. Then a young woman emerged from the cabin. She was wearing a red bikini. She shouted towards Edmond, "Catching anything?"

"No, nothing so far!"

"Do you mind if I take a picture of you and your boat. I am working on a calendar for the government of Martinique," she said with a pronounced French accent.

Edmond felt relieved. "Of course! Take whatever photographs you want." He turned away from the camera as she began to take a rapid series of photographs. He adjusted his fisherman's cap to shield his face. Even though he had not shaved in three days, he was still recognizable.

He continued pretending to bait his hooks, using another flying fish that had leaped aboard the vessel in the early morning hours. Edmond had always loved to fish so his actions were fluid and natural.

Turning away from the cigarette boat, he whispered to Magdalene, "I would have never thought that we would attract such interest. I agree with you – there is something strange about all of this. It is not inconceivable that the aircraft has radioed our location and a description of our vessel. Even as we speak, they may be verifying our images via digital scan in Barbados. A woman in a red bikini does not make sense. Why don't the rest of the crew show themselves?"

Magdalene did not immediately reply. After a moment she lifted the tarpaulin. "It is so hot under the tarp. How much longer do you think before she finishes taking pictures?"

Suddenly, the engines of the cigarette boat revved up. It slowly moved and began to circle their vessel once more. The invisible crew seemed to be observing them. It was apparent that they were awaiting instructions.

Then, the cigarette boat lunged forward, its engines given maximum throttle. The wake rocked the sloop furiously. Edmond lost his balance and dropped his fishing gear as he fell.

As he struggled to get up, he said, "They must think we are indeed fishermen otherwise they would have attempted to board us. They apparently failed to identify us, or at least I pray so."

Magdalene emerged from under the tarpaulin. "What makes you so certain they failed to identify the boat and you? As you know, all they had to do was read *Sea Dreams* on the stern plate ."

"Well, one thing worked in our favor and maybe saved our lives. I painted over the name of the boat early this morning before you awoke. I found some black paint in the cuddy and changed the name into a floral design."

"Edmond, the more I am with you, the more I become impressed. I will remember you in my prayers."

"You pray?"

"Yes, I do. I want to be a good person."

"Do you go to confession?"

"No, my religion is not the same as yours. I will not trust anyone with my secrets."

Late in the evening before the sky turned to the colors of twilight, they spotted two small islands just off the bow. To starboard was a larger island. Overhead they could see various airplanes heading towards it. The hills were not distinct and the topography offered few clues as to the identity of the island.

The island to port, however, was easily recognizable. While smaller, it possessed a unique landmark. Smoke wafted from the southern end of the island, reaching towards the sky.

"Magdalene, there's our destination. The Soufrière Hills volcano makes Montserrat easy to identify."

"You are a great navigator and sailor!" she said, smiling.

"I should be, the U.S. Navy spent a fortune training me."

"Take some credit for yourself. You may have been trained for such a task, but not to protect me."

"What choice did I have? Remember, they are after me, too."

"Ann told me several things about the island that you need to know. There's no way to dock at the port city of Plymouth since it was destroyed by the volcano. We have to sail around to the northeastern side of the island where there is unfortunately not sufficient docking to accommodate us."

"I did not know the volcano is still so active. There is much more smoke being emitted than I would have thought," said Edmond. "I just hope there is sufficient holding ground for us to anchor close in."

Edmond looked closely at the topography of the island. It appeared to be two islands, one of desolation and the other of tropical beauty. "The danger is not the smoke, but the fact that the volcanic dome of the mountain appears to have been rebuilt. The time will come when it will explode again casting pyroclastic flows across the landscape. In other words, steam, stones and lava will come forth and rain on anyone foolish enough to be in the southern sector of the island. Only the northeastern quadrant of the island is still safe."

As *Sea Dreams* rounded the island, they could see what had happened to Plymouth and the other settlements built too close to the smoldering gateway to hell. They were now communities buried in stone.

"After hearing about the island during the cruise, I went to the ship's library and found some old VHS tapes. Can you believe that? If I remember from the documentary made a few years ago, over sixty percent of the island is an exclusion zone. No one can enter that section of the island unless they have permission and are accompanied by the police. Of course, my authority for this information was probably produced by some travel channel. There was an entire series on the island, otherwise I would have known absolutely nothing about it. I can't believe I am actually here, almost swimming distance away."

"Edmond, it must be true that Ann's family has moved to the northern part of the island. It should not be that difficult to locate them. After all, the island is not that large."

Magdalene scanned the island with the field glasses that her uncle had left on the boat. "The northern part of Montserrat appears to be covered in tropical forest. It is possible to hide very easily in such an environment."

"How much do you know about her family?" asked Edmond.

"Only what Ann told me. Their last name is O'Dea. They came to Montserrat about thirty years ago from Ireland. Her father was a hotel manager in Plymouth. At that time, Plymouth was very popular with expatriates, especially the Irish."

Edmond recalled what he learned from the cassettes about the island. "But with the explosion of the Soufriere Hills volcano, all of that ended. The perfect Georgian settlement was buried under ten feet of pumice. The European way of life ended for the upper class. Plymouth was buried in 40 feet of volcanic mud. The volcano has once more developed a dome and is showing that there is still pyroclastic activity. There are many guesses as to when she will erupt again."

"Ann said her parents live in Saint Peter Parish on the northwest coast of the island. The other two parishes are just too dangerous for people to live in. I can't imagine anyone living under such a threat."

"This evening I will attempt to anchor us in Little Bay," said Edmond with a degree of caution in his voice. "The capital of the island is being relocated there. It is not my boat to destroy, but I suggest we remove all identifying marks from the boat after dark. Then I will tie the helm down and send her seaward towards the Gulf of Mexico. It is the only way we can avoid being questioned. If we are lucky, the authorities will show little interest in us when we will tell them that we arrived on *Caribe Queen,* the ferry from Antigua after flying from Puerto Rico. If you are correct, the pursuers do not expect us to fly to Antigua."

As the afternoon faded into early evening, Edmond heard the thrashing of a shark. Occasionally its head would pound the wooden hull. It was a particularly large fish. It had probably been following them for a day or so hoping to receive a tribute from a fisherman. Magdalene and Edmond watched the shark's dorsal fin submerge only to reappear followed by a pounding against the hull of the boat.

"Edmond, it is not good to see a shark on the last day of a voyage. What if we need to swim ashore? Will it attack us?"

"It is probably only a bull shark, more curious than intent on devouring us. Besides you are not superstitious are you?"

"If you mean careful, yes, I am. By the way, how do we get ashore this evening? There is no wharf and the cliffs are very steep along the oceanfront. In fact, I don't even see a beach."

"We will have to find the safest place to land. Carr's or Little Bay represent some possibilities. Shark or no shark, we are going to have to swim to the beach after I lash the helm."

"Are you sure we have to abandon the boat? Isn't there another way?" Magdalene asked.

"We must do what we have to in order to survive. As you know, there is nowhere else to flee to. Once found, the boat will serve as a link to us. Besides, if they find the boat abandoned in the middle of the Gulf of Mexico, they will assume that we suffered a mishap. It is best that they think we are already dead."

Edmond glanced towards the tiller. "I will put a weak knot in the line. It will eventually work its way free. With the direction of the wind, the vessel will travel east, southeast."

Chapter 5
WHERE DREAMS AND LIES MEET

The dark comes too quickly in the tropics. The twilight lingers but a moment. In the distance they could hear the wind blowing through the fronds of the palm trees. Large breakers fell upon the rocks, the entrance to the bay barely protected from the onslaught of the sea.

The draft of the sailboat was just a little over four feet. They would have to go over the side before swimming and then wading ashore. They decided to bring only one backpack with them. Anything more would have garnered the suspicion of the island police.

They entered the warm sea and clung to the stern of the boat before letting go. They tried to touch the bottom but the depth was too great. "We need to let go now and swim for the shore. Try to keep your movements fluid, not erratic. That way we do not attract the shark."

They began their journey towards the shore. Even though Magdalene tried to swim slowly, the fear within her rose. Her strokes became more frantic as did her kicks. Edmond held back, ready to protect her should the shark attack.

Soon their feet touched the shell-strewn bottom of the

shoreline. They crawled ashore and then turned on their backs, facing the myriad stars above them. They did not speak as they lay side by side on the sand. Their breathing slowed to a normal pace. Edmond took Magdalene's hand and gently held it. She turned towards him, smiled and then closed her eyes.

Edmond could not believe that the shark did not attack them. He realized that they might have encountered a riptide, too. He was thankful to be alive and to be with her.

In the darkness, they walked slowly for a short distance, then rested once more beneath the coconut palms that lined the beach. Soon they fell asleep. Edmond held Magdalene close to him. In his embrace she felt safe, perhaps for the first time in her life. He had not held a woman close to him since April's disappearance.

He recalled the events in Ireland that created this moment in time. Then the strange Facebook messages that led him to Magdalene and Montserrat. He did not believe in coincidences. He wondered if there was a link between April's disappearance and Ann Pennington's attempts to connect with him through Facebook.

Soon he too was asleep. In his dream, he saw April emerging from the sea. At first she was surrounded by the spray of falling breakers. Then as she neared him, she held her arms out to embrace him. Just as he reached for her, a loud noise awakened him. Trembling, he sat up quickly, Magdalene falling from the safety of his arms. "What was that crashing sound?" he whispered far too loudly.

She turned towards him and laughed. "What you heard was the thud of a coconut falling. We are fortunate it did not hit us. The strong wind must have loosened it. One of us could have been killed if we had been hit directly."

"From now on, I will look above me when deciding on a place to sleep. The only coconut trees I know are found in four-star resorts where coconuts do not fall on sleeping tourists during the night," Edmond said, laughing.

They moved away from the grove of swaying trees and waited for the first signs of the dawn. They did not want to appear as vagrants sleeping on the beach. They were careful to straighten their clothing so as to look like they just arrived on the island. Edmond wished he could shave. "I have never tried to dress in the dark much less shave myself by moonlight. I guess it is best that I don't have a change of clothing or a razor nearby. Perhaps I will look even more like a scholar with a beard and wrinkled clothes," he said, dusting the now dried sand from his pants.

As the sun broke free from the surface of the sea, they walked slowly inland to a small village that clung to a cliff above the bay. Already, it was alive with activity as fisherman prepared to depart for the sea below them. Others stared at Magdalene and Edmond in silence, wondering what two visitors were doing there so early in the morning.

They ignored the questioning looks of the residents. After a while, an older fisherman approached them carrying some tackle in one hand and a bait bucket in the other. "Good morning," said Edmond. "We are looking for the O'Dea family. Can you tell us where they live?"

"They live everywhere," he responded.

"I am sorry. What do you mean *everywhere*?" asked Edmond.

There are a lots of O'Deas on the island."

"Oh, I am sorry. This family has fair skin and looks very Irish. Their daughter Ann was born here."

"Don't know anyone that looks like they recently arrived from Ireland. I think you have the wrong century in mind. If the year is 1670, I might be able to take you to the right person. We are all black Irish," he said, laughing.

"Thank you. I guess I will have to pretend that it is 1670," Edmond said with a forced smile.

Edmond looked at Magdalene. "I am afraid I don't feel like being humorous today."

"Edmond, try to relax. How could he have known that you just 'evolved' from the sea?" she said with a laugh.

They continued walking for a while, then Magdalene suggested they rest. Sitting on a stone wall under a lime tree, they looked at the lush tropical forest and the ever-present smoke rising from the volcano. The mountain demanded that a person not forget its presence. Thoughts and conversations revolved around it. The only active volcano that Edmond had seen before was when his ship had steamed up Tokyo Wan towards the port of Yokosuka, Japan. Nameless mountains emitted billowing white smoke that rose across the windswept bay.

His thoughts continued to be drawn to the mountain of pyroclastic flow. As they sat on the stone wall, they could sense the earth breathing. A light smell of sulfur drifted in the air, then vanished, replaced by the sweet breath of blooming bougainvillea.

"My feet hurt and I am very hungry," said Magdalene as she messaged her foot that had been bruised and slightly cut by coral.

The rich aroma of something good cooking drifted in the air. "Let's see where that great smell is coming from. Seeing the limes on these trees, I would love a lime drink with plenty of alcohol in it," said Edmond, who was more thirsty than hungry.

They walked down a path towards the Dripping Water Café that was surrounded by banana plants and breadfruit trees. They sat down at a brightly painted table and waited to be served in the open-air restaurant. Soft-drink caps, used as checkers, littered the table.

A young woman approached them. "What you want to eat and drink?" she said musically.

Edmond smiled at her. "I want what smells so good."

"You want goat water? It's local stew. My mother makes the best on the island of Montserrat. My parents owned the grandest restaurant in Plymouth before the eruption. Expats loved to eat there. Famous recording artists used to sit at the bar, but that is all gone now, forever gone."

"It must have been quite a spectacle. I understand that Plymouth was a beautiful capital with its blend of traditional and Georgian architectures. It saddens me to think that so much beauty is lost," said Edmond, smiling at her.

"I like you. You nice man," said the young girl.

"I wish you were right about the nice part. It is kind of you to say it, anyway."

"What you doing in Dripping Water?" she asked with a questioning smile.

"Is that the name of your village?" asked Magdalene, who had been ignored until now.

"Yes, there is a small waterfall just down the path where the water is very warm."

Edmond smiled at Magdalene. "Fresh warm water! You know what I am thinking?"

The server remained waiting for them to complete their order. "What you drink?"

"Anything with limes in it as long as there is more alcohol than water," Edmond said seriously.

"Dripping water punch is what you want. It will awaken a dead man."

"Perfect. Make that two dripping water punches," Edmond said, looking at Magdalene.

The food and drinks had a profound medicinal effect on them. The depression and pain left their bodies after only two drinks. The strong rum gave them a sense of security. The food nourished their tired bodies, making them even sleepier as they sat in the warm tropical sun. The sound of wild canaries added to the serenity that now surrounded them if only for a moment.

Magdalene and Edmond remained silent as they stretched out their legs and basked in the warm wind of the sea. They watched the distant sail of a small boat below them as it headed away from the island.

"Do you think that is *Sea Dreams*?" asked Magdalene.

"Yes, it is. I recognize the single reef that I put in the sail and the long bowsprit. At least it has cleared the island. Hopefully, whoever is watching for us will think that we did not come ashore on Montserrat, and that we are now heading towards another destination. Of course, I can only hope that."

"I am sad to think that my uncle's boat will soon be lost. After the cigarette boat and the airplane, I think we made a wise decision."

Soon the stew was served. The steamy well-seasoned

goat water was excellent. He remembered one of his sailing magazines saying that it was a person's appetite that determined the pleasure of any food. Before long their glasses were refilled with dripping water punch again. There was far more rum than lime, but that only added to the flavor. He had never tasted such a tantalizing drink.

Looking towards the server who was now washing dishes just a short distance from their table, he said, "We are looking for an Irish family, the O'Deas. They came to the island around thirty years ago."

"I knew an Irish family in Plymouth with that name. I don't know what happened to them. Like all of us, they had to flee either to England or to the northwest corner of the island. I attended a private school with Ann, their daughter."

"I knew Ann!" said Magdalene, unable to hide her enthusiasm.

"Do you know what happened to her?" ask Edmond, hoping to gain more information.

"She go to England and became a doctor," the server responded.

"Really? Where does she practice?"

"I don't know. After the eruption of Soufriere Hills, I have not seen her parents."

Edmond whispered to Magdalene, "The parents must have known what she did for a living or they would not have made up such a lie."

"What is wrong with what Ann and I do for a living?" Magdalene asked loudly, the rum having removed her inhibitions.

"I did not mean to imply that what you are doing is

wrong. It is just not what a person does regardless of how unfortunate they are."

"It is our body, not yours or the government's," Magdalene said angrily.

"I am sorry. A person needs to be free to choose what course in life to take." Edmond felt awkward arguing about prostitution. However, he realized that life was not inherently fair to everyone, especially those who found themselves unable to escape poverty or the prejudices of others.

They left the café and walked up a lane that soon turned steep and stony. Above them was a brick church. Outside, a priest was digging in the soil of a small garden surrounded by a low stone wall.

"Good morning, Father," said Edmond as they approached.

The priest, who was preparing to plant roses, raised himself up from a squatting position. "Who says good morning to me?" he said with a warm smile. His Irish accent was very strong.

"Father, two tourists who wish you a beautiful day."

"Thank you, my son. I don't believe I have seen you two on the island before. Can I help you? Perhaps a recommendation regarding where to stay or my favorite café?"

"That is very kind of you, Father. We are day campers who arrived with the ferry. A recommendation from you on where to stay would be most appreciated. I think we have already found the best café."

"And what café might that be?"

"The Dripping Water. We had the goat-water stew and an excellent drink or two. I believe Montserrat has the best limes among all the islands that we have visited."

"So, you met Mary. She is a fine person. One of my parishioners. You may not know it but her family owned one of the finest restaurants in Plymouth. That is before the mountain vented its anger."

The priest continued, "Regarding a place to stay, I would suggest the Dubliner's Inn. It is down the lane just a short distance. James O'Brien and his wife own it. They migrated from Ireland just a few years ago. It is nice to see people who come from the same home island. You see, I am from the west coast of Ireland, too. County Galway, that is."

"Father, we are looking for the Irish O'Dea family. We knew their daughter Ann. We were hoping to drop by and say hello."

The priest turned ashen. Edmond noticed that his hands trembled. "I don't know any O'Dea family. Never heard of an Ann O'Dea on this island. Are they relatives of yours?"

"No, we only know Ann. She is such a fine person with her beautiful red hair, and her smile would render light to the day," said Edmond.

The priest continued to look concerned. "I haven't heard of her, but you and your wife might want to have confession."

"No, Father, not today."

"Are you so certain of life that your sins can wait? There is never a convenient time."

Edmond sensed that the priest knew more about the O'Dea family and Ann than he was willing to admit. It was as though he had a secret he was entrusted to guard.

He looked once more at Edmond. "Now, young man, what brought you and your young wife to Montserrat? Was it the O'Dea family or something else? You seem like a scholar to me. A sociologist, biologist or some other professorship?" Edmond did not reply. The priest continued, "Because of the frequent volcanic eruptions, not to mention Hurricane Hugo, most of what tourists came here to see has vanished. As you know over half the island is an exclusion zone. There is nothing for tourists here to see or experience that cannot be found in Antigua. Here only the danger remains."

"I guess I did not answer your question," responded Edmond. "I hate to repeat myself, but we came specifically to see the O'Dea family."

"It is a strange coincidence, but just yesterday two visitors were asking me if anyone had stopped by looking for the O'Dea family. Were those two visitors related to your search?"

"No, they were not." Edmond paused. "Did they mention looking for anyone in particular?"

"They asked whether someone new had arrived on Montserrat. It is just like outsiders to assume that I know everyone who comes and goes on the island. I told them that we have a ferry and helicopter flights in and out of the island. People can come and go without my knowing about it. We also get a lot of fishermen from other islands stopping by for fuel and other supplies. It seems like boats never carry enough water. They know we have excellent fresh water that comes from the springs deep within the earth."

"Father, I would appreciate you not mentioning us to anyone or the fact that we are seeking the O'Deas. When we find them, we want it to be a total surprise."

"You need not worry. I know how fast news can travel on this island. Since we live simply, we have little to do but talk.

By the way, don't forget to go to confession, my son. We all need God's help."

"I won't forget. Thank you for your kindness," responded Edmond.

Magdalene and Edmond continued walking down the tree-lined path that broadened as it descended from the small church building. On either side of the lane, people stared at them but did not speak. Their curiosity was apparent, however, in their faces.

Soon they were standing in front of the Dubliner's Inn. It was a small two-story edifice. It stood out in that it was not made of cinder block with exterior plaster that was common among commercial buildings and more substantial dwellings. Instead, the building seemed colonial in appearance. The roof was corrugated metal that had once been painted bright red, but had now lost its luster in the tropic heat and frequent showers of the island. The building itself was made of wood with faded green shutters. Breadfruit and banana plants adorned the front and side yards providing a degree of privacy while giving a view of the sea from the front and side porches.

Like in many gardens in the tropics, coconut trees and bright multicolored bougainvillea were in abundance. A very sweet smell drifted in the light air, intoxicating in its allurement.

Magdalene looked towards Edmond. "Let's stay here. My feet hurt, and I am exhausted. I am sure that the priest and Mary would not have misled us in their recommendation to stay here. I wish we had taken the time to dip in the hot water of that spring Mary mentioned. If we had, I believe I would now be feeling much better."

"I agree with you," responded Edmond. "The warm waters fed by the thermal heat of a volcano are known to be helpful for a variety of conditions, especially aching muscles." He looked at her with a smile that conveyed his empathy. "I think we have traveled far enough for today. Even though it is still early afternoon, I am way too tired to go further. The lack of sleep and the climb up the cliff, then our walk up and down the hill have taken all of my energy. The thought of sleep is overpowering."

As they approached the inn, they could hear soft music coming from inside the gaily trimmed colorful building. A CD of Enya's was heard oozing from the mahogany bar. Her haunting voice seemed in conflict with the tropical nature of the inn where Bob Marley's "Redemption Song" seemed more appropriate.

After entering they could smell liquor combined with stale cigarette smoke even though prominently displayed was a SMOKE FREE INN sign. Islanders had a tendency to bend the rules.

A red-faced overweight man in his fifties approached them from behind the bar. He was wearing a cook's apron. "What can I do for you two? A room, drink or a meal?" It was apparent that the inn had a very small staff.

After some hesitation, Edmond looked at Magdalene. "My wife and I would like a room for tonight. One with an ocean view if available."

"All our rooms have ocean views," the innkeeper said in an unwelcoming voice. "We don't have any air-conditioning, so the trade winds and the shade of our trees act as our cooling system."

"Sounds like a writer's ideal place to stay. This inn has plenty of atmosphere," said Edmond to Magdalene as she pressed herself against him.

"We don't have any single beds. Will a double with a private bath do?"

Edmond looked at Magdalene. "Of course, unless my wife objects. We have only been married a short time, but she says my snoring keeps her awake. I probably need to get one of those CPAP machines for sleep apnea, but my wife says they are not very romantic."

Magdalene laughed. "As long as you don't get intimate with me, I am okay with it."

The innkeeper smiled at Magdalene. "There is always the couch if your husband becomes a problem. Of course, you can always call me," he said with an exaggerated wink.

James O'Brien led them to the last room on the second floor. The walls were painted a light sky blue while the ceiling was Honduran mahogany. As they entered, the curtains were gently moving in the breeze. There were no window screens so protection from the insect population depended on the flimsy mosquito netting suspended above the four-poster. The bed and furniture were stained a dark color and appeared to be hand-carved from mahogany.

After showing them the bathroom, James asked, "Will this do for you? As you may have noticed, the balcony is private. It is the only room in the inn with such a feature."

"Before we get too enthusiastic, how much is the room per night?"

"Two hundred East Caribbean dollars. We don't take credit cards. If you have traveler's checks, that will be fine."

"I don't have East Caribbean dollars, but I do have U.S. currency. Will that do?"

"Of course, we are not prejudiced against outsiders. Anyone from a country that warred against the British is always welcome here."

After James left, Edmond looked at Magdalene. "I am glad they only take cash. It is too easy to trace credit cards."

"Well, I am going to take a bath and then lie down. It is difficult not to know what lies ahead for us. I cannot say enough about how indebted I am to you for staying with me. I would probably have died by now if not for you." She paused and looked into his eyes. "Is there anything special I can do for you tonight?"

Edmond knew what she meant. He longed to answer her with an embrace but hesitated. "Magdalene, I want you very much. More so than I have desired anyone since the disappearance of my wife. You are very beautiful and innocent, but not now. Not tonight. I still love April and my love for her has not diminished. I would feel that I was betraying her if we had sex. If we made love, I would then be indebted to you, and I don't want that to occur, at least not yet. Our lives are too much in jeopardy to become emotionally involved." Edmond knew that pure reason did not apply in the relationship between a man and a woman. The nature of man is not one of obedience to any rule whether made by man or God. He knew that nothing could repress desire.

She looked away and then smiled as she began to unpack her suitcase. She realized that she now controlled him just as a puppet master commanded a doll. Magdalene knew that eventually his desire for her would prevail if not tonight then soon.

As she undressed, Edmond could not help but observe her. He was surprised at how worn her clothing was. It looked like items purchased from a thrift store in the States. It was apparent that she had not been working in the brothel long enough to have accumulated enough money to purchase the gaudy costumes of her trade.

He could hear her singing accompanied by the splashing of water as she bathed. It was a soft voice yet pure in tone.

He walked out onto the veranda where the fans moved slowly. Soon he heard her speak to him. "Edmond, I will lie down now. You can join me if you like."

"No, I will sit here on the veranda and look at the sea. It is very peaceful out here." He did not wish to violate his own self-imposed rules for he knew how much he was attracted to her. As he looked at the sea framed by two large breadfruit trees, his eyes began to feel heavy. He walked over to a chair and leaned his head back. The large leaves of the garden trees protected his eyes from the sun. Soon he too was asleep. A sleep nurtured by the warm Caribbean Sea breeze.

He awoke two hours later, startled as he felt an insect biting his cheek. His neck hurt for he had slept at an awkward angle. Edmond heard Magdalene walking towards his chair.

He looked at her. "I have never seen you more beautiful than you are now."

"Thank you. A clean bathrobe certainly helped, not to mention two hours of sleep. I see you could not stay awake either."

Below, they could hear James in the kitchen. The smell of fish frying alerted their senses to the fact that they had not eaten in several hours. "Let's go down to the bar and order a Funky Monkey, my favorite drink. I discovered it in St. Lucia when April and I stayed there for a week years ago. It was the hotel bar's specialty."

"What on earth is in it?" Magdalene asked.

"If I remember correctly, lots of rum and a little chocolate. But I am sure it has more ingredients than those."

Soon they were pulling chairs back from the small counter that served as the bar. "James, once we finish our drinks, I want to order whatever you have been frying. It smells delicious."

"I have been cooking some flying fish for myself."

Magdalene and Edmond looked at each other. They immediately thought of Barbados where the flying fish had national significance.

"James," said Edmond, "I would like to know more about Saint Patrick's Day. I can't believe that a Caribbean island would celebrate that day as a national holiday. I also understand that Montserrat is called the Emerald Isle in recognition of its ties to Ireland. I assume that the history of your country reflects this mutual respect."

James looked at them while he served the Funky Monkeys. "That's only for tourists. The truth is very different. As you know, Cromwell gave the Irish hell in the 1600s. Those he did not have killed were sent to the Caribbean as slaves to work in the sugarcane and cotton fields. Along with the Irish were Africans for whom he also had little regard. Many of the slaves, both black and white, were sent to Barbados. Later, when slavery ended for the Irish, it continued for the blacks. While many Irish and blacks had children together, the freed Irish did not look upon their fellow African slaves as free men. Instead, the Irish in Montserrat enslaved them just as the English had previously done. Eventually, the Africans began to organize a rebellion against their new taskmasters. Fortunately for the Irish, the word got out that a rebellion was in the works.

"The Irish wanted to make an example of those who no longer wished to be slaves. So, on Saint Patrick's Day they hanged several Africans who had plotted the revolt as examples to others. So you see, what the Island celebrates is not the driving of snakes out of Ireland but the execution of their fellow Montserratians. It is strange how freely the past is manipulated for commercial gain – in this case, the tourist industry."

"I guess there is still animosity towards outsiders on the island?" asked Edmond.

"Not really, we love their money too much."

Edmond wished to change the subject. "I hope we are not interfering with your meal. The only place that I have heard of where people consider the flying fish a delicacy is Barbados. Have you spent much time there?"

"Occasionally I go there to see friends. My girlfriend also lives on the island. My wife lives here on Montserrat."

Before Magdalene could ask the name of his girlfriend, Edmond interrupted, "We have never been to Barbados. Would you recommend it to tourists?"

"Absolutely, especially to single men," he said with a smile. "The women there are very beautiful."

"Well, that leaves me out. We are on our honeymoon. Maggie and I were married in Puerto Rico just a couple of weeks ago. By the way, my name is Phillip."

"For you two tourists, I will make the dish that the inn is internationally known for: Mountain Chicken."

"That sounds great. I couldn't help but admire the mangos growing in the garden."

James walked over to a nearby tree and pulled two fruit from it. "These are called Julie mangos. Their origin is here in the Caribbean. They are the sweetest in the world." He handed them to Edmond.

After cutting into the flesh of the colorful fruit, Magdalene said, "I agree, I have never tasted a mango so good before."

James looked at her. "I think you are pulling my leg. I bet you have been to these islands before. There is something about your accent that makes me think you are from here."

Edmond frowned. "You are mistaking a southern accent for a Barbadian one. Southerners are often confused with Australians and New Zealanders. So you see, my wife's accent is not as local as you may think."

James smiled as though they were all sharing a secret.

After finishing their meal, Edmond suggested to Magdalene that they take a walk since they had eaten so much. "Magdalene, I don't feel comfortable about staying at this inn. I think James knows more than he is telling. When I went to the restroom, I noticed that he has a shortwave radio sitting in an anteroom just off the kitchen. He can communicate with boats, planes and even other countries. I believe we can only trust the priest and no one else."

They reached the rise where the church stood and saw the parish house where the priest lived. It was a small white cinder-block building that had plaster on the outside. Edmond knocked on the door. When the priest opened the door, Edmond asked, "Father, may we talk with you?"

"Certainly. You are both welcome here, please come in. I get very lonely at times. Religion is not as important to Montserratians as it once was." The large casement windows were open, allowing the wind to enter. The small room had a desk and three wooden chairs. Crucifixes hung from the walls, Saint Bridget's cross prominently displayed among them.

"As we mentioned before, we are looking for the O'Dea family. Magdalene knew Ann O'Dea when she was a student."

"Tragic story," the priest responded. "She had just finished medical school before she was killed in an avalanche in Nepal. She and her new husband were determined to climb that cursed mountain, Mt. Everest. A shame, she had so much to offer the sick. I don't think her parents ever got over it. Before her death, her parents worshipped here. Faithful people in attendance until their beloved daughter died."

Edmond looked at Magdalene. "Father, I am not sure we are talking about the same person."

"I am sorry if we are not. Ann started her medical career at the University of Barbados before transferring to a university in England. I only assumed that was the time in which your wife and Ann might have known each another."

"Is it possible for us to offer our condolences to the O'Deas in person?" asked Edmond.

"Of course. I will draw you a map on how to reach them." The priest began to sketch the northwestern part of the island.

"This is just a rough map of the area, but hopefully it will be accurate enough. You will not have any problem in finding them if you follow my directions. If you do, just ask someone along the road. They will help you."

"Father," said Edmond, "please do not share our inquiry with anyone. We want to surprise them."

"Of course, I am certain they will enjoy a visit especially from someone that knew Ann."

Upon arriving back at the inn, they found dust masks and a page of instructions regarding their use. Edmond read the instructions out loud to Magdalene. "In the event of ash, close all doors and windows. If you venture outside, please wear the protective face mask."

Edmond laughed. "I have never seen instructions like these before in a hotel. I wonder if you can go and see the volcano? If so, it would make a beautiful sight at night."

"That would be exciting," Magdalene said with a smile.

As they walked down the stairs to ask James about viewing the volcano, they stepped quietly so as not to disturb another guest who appeared to be sleeping in a chair, his head resting at an awkward angle.

They could hear James speaking softly to someone in the small alcove off the kitchen. "Yah, I am telling you it might be them." A pause followed as he listened to the recipient of his call. Then softly he said, "I know! I know!" Then he stopped transmitting as if he sensed their presence.

"Oh, excuse me. I was just talking to a friend of mine, Lou Maitre, about three Blackbelly sheep I found grazing on my pasture just up the hill from here. Lou doesn't think they are his. The frequent tremors caused by the volcano have made it difficult to keep property fenced."

"Blackbelly sheep? Did you buy them in Barbados?" asked Edmond. He remembered Pamela, his guide, pointing out their unusual traits when he had first arrived in Barbados. "If I remember correctly, they are virtually hairless with black bellies."

"Yes, that is correct. I have no idea why or where Lou bought them. He likes to keep his business deals a secret. Of course, nothing is kept a secret in Montserrat. This island possesses eyes that cannot be seen, only felt."

Edmond looked again at James. "Is it possible for us to see the volcano at night? It must be most beautiful when it is dark. It would really please Maggie if we could view it when its colors are most vivid."

"Yes, I can drive you to Jack Boy Hill where there is a great view. You'll be able to see the lights of Antigua as well as Guadeloupe in the distance. If we are lucky, you two will be treated to a display of fire and cascading molten rock. If not, you will see only ash. It will cost you 30 East Caribbean dollars each. Are you interested?"

"The answer is yes if you will take us both there for 50 East Caribbean dollars," Magdalene said with the conviction of an auctioneer.

"Your young wife is a good trader." James laughed. "Are you sure she is not from the islands?"

Later that evening, James pulled up to the entrance to the inn in an old Jeep Wagoneer convertible. Edmond wondered where he got the parts to keep it running. The fumes from the rough running engine served to discourage the mosquitoes that were biting Edmond and Magdalene as they sat on the porch waiting for James.

The drive to Jack Boy hill was bumpy yet it was exhilarating in the open-air vehicle especially after their bath and nap. The clear night sky was filled with stars. Occasionally they would get a glimpse of the volcano, and then the silhouettes of the trees would hide the cauldron of fire and molten rock.

The road ended at a small dimly lit souvenir shop. Inside, a Montserratian glared at them as they entered to look around. "I am used to clerks smiling even if most of the clientele turn out to be nothing more than window shoppers," said Edmond as they walked down the narrow aisles. The shop contained the usual display of carved coconuts and handmade items. Plastic volcanoes made in China also lined the shelves as well as locally collected seashells. Next to the shop was a telescope and restroom that were available for a nominal charge.

As they left the shop, Magdalene asked Edmond, "Do you mind if I spend your money looking at the volcano? I have never seen one before."

Edmond smiled at her. "Of course not. Take your time."

They both stood looking towards the pyroclastic glow. Above the heart of the volcano, thick billowing opaque smoke could be seen silhouetted by the rising moon. The mountain seemed to pulsate as though the earth were exhaling breaths of fire.

As Magdalene watched the display, she began to tremble. Edmond put his hand in hers and squeezed it. "Are you feeling ill?"

"No, just afraid. God seems so indifferent here on this island. It is like witnessing the painful birth of the earth. No one is safe here. On this island, good and evil can perish together at any moment. The buried capital, villages and farms are hidden from us in the night."

Edmond paused. "We did not see the loss of so many lives. We only see the beauty of the night now. We can only imagine the fury of the volcano's eruption. So many people do not plan for what must eventually happen." Edmond put his arm around her and held her close. Her trembling was now gone.

He then looked for James whom he had not seen since their arrival. Edmond went into the souvenir shop and asked the attendant, "I am looking for our driver. Have you seen him?"

"James? No," replied the clerk, avoiding eye contact.

Edmond walked outside of the souvenir shop and looked around. He could hear James talking on his satellite phone, "I tell you it is them. No, wait. Listen to what I am saying. Okay, how long before . . ." A long silence ensued when he noticed Edmond staring at him.

"Had to call my wife. She never understands when I am late coming home. She thinks I am with another woman. Here in Montserrat, men often have one or more mistresses. Most wives understand that but not mine. Why do men marry?" he said with a weak laugh.

Edmond did not respond to the question, yet he knew the answer.

As Edmond and the innkeeper approached Magdalene,

James quickly asked, "Would you like a rum punch? Perhaps a souvenir?" He seemed very nervous as though he were expecting something to happen. It was apparent that he wanted to delay their departure.

"No, I do not want a drink," replied Magdalene. "I want to remember this night just as it is for the rest of my life."

Becoming even more nervous, James paced as he listened to Magdalene's refusal. Only Edmond seemed to notice his strange behavior.

The jeep swerved into some sharp curves as they descended through the jungle. Soon they entered a clear stretch of road where sugarcane and cotton grew, then reentered the thick jungle. Illuminated by the headlights of the jeep, two men were walking rapidly towards them. Each man positioned themselves on opposite sides of the road, holding a cutlass – a long curved blade used to harvest banana stalks and to cut into the hard shells of the coconut.

Edmond's grip on Magdalene's hand tightened. He whispered, "As soon as the jeep slows down, jump off the tailgate and run into the jungle as quickly as you can. Do not hesitate to follow my lead and be sure not speak until we are safe in the underbrush."

As the jeep approached the two men, James began to slow down. In the dim lights of the jeep, the men appeared featureless. The men lunged toward the vehicle as soon as it reached them.

Edmond and Magdalene leaped off the back of the jeep and ran into the darkness. After a short distance, they both fell off the embankment and rolled down a small hill until they came to rest against the foliage. Cut and bruised, they waited, listening for sounds of their pursuers. They did not speak, only their breathing could be heard. Soon the noises of the jungle returned.

As they remained motionless and silent, they heard James shouting loudly, "Phillip, Maggie, come back to the jeep. What's wrong with you two? The men you saw said that they had been working late at a nearby banana plantation and were on their way home. They didn't mean to scare you so badly. Phillip! Maggie!"

They could hear James and the two men talking but could not make out what was being said. Soon they saw the beams of three flashlights that indicated that the searchers were running down the road looking for them. In the darkness, they assumed that their prey would have taken the easiest path to escape.

Edmond whispered to Magdalene, "We need to stay here until early dawn. The moment there's enough light to see, we need to move as quickly as we can, avoiding detection if possible. I hear water flowing nearby. We can drink from it."

"Do you think they are still searching for us?" asked Magdalene. "Perhaps James was right. They could have been tired workers wanting a ride home."

"I don't know, but my instinct tells me we did the right thing."

"What about our room and the few things we left there? I left my backpack behind with my only change of panties in it," she said.

"If I am correct about us being in danger, then it really

does not matter. After all, we didn't bring that much with us to begin with. If I am wrong about James, he will keep everything for us. The only problem we would then have will be one hell of a hotel bill."

As they waited, the insects hummed about them as strange animals made monkey-like sounds in the rain forest. Then a light rain began to fall. It was soon followed by a heavy shower. In what seemed like just a moment, the sounds of the night forest vanished as twilight stalked across the mountains.

"I am certainly glad I brought my wallet and passport with me. Did you bring your purse with you?"

"Yes, I did. I slung it over my shoulder when we jumped." She paused and then looked away. "Please forgive how I look," she said as she matted down her rain-soaked hair. Her short denim skirt and white blouse were the color of volcanic ash. Yet in the twilight, she was more beautiful than she had been to him. The makeup that concealed her natural beauty was removed by the rain and replaced with the skin tone of youth.

Edmond continued to look at her. "I have the map that the priest gave us in my pocket. If we are lucky, we can follow it once we locate a crossroad. In the meantime, the morning star will give us a rough course to follow. At least we will know if we are heading north towards the O'Deas or south into the exclusion zone. We certainly do not want to get any closer to the volcano than we have to. The amount of falling ash tells me that the volcano continues to be restless. Last night I could feel the earth trembling beneath me while I tried to sleep."

As they walked, at times limping from their bruised and now tender feet, they followed a small stream that ran parallel to the road but attempted to remain a safe distance from it in case someone was tracking them. The pursuers knew that in the heat and humidity of the jungle, thirst would soon become an issue. Careless people would closely follow the stream in pursuit of water and as a point of bearing.

Occasionally, their clothes would become entangled in sharp thorns or the lower branches of a tree. "If we continue to travel like this," said Magdalene, "we will both be naked and covered in blood before we arrive at the O'Dea house. They will then be afraid to let us in, and I would not blame them."

"I don't think we have any alternatives," said Edmond as he swatted biting flies that congregated near the waters of the stream. "We have abundant water but no food to provide us with energy."

Magdalene stopped and frowned at Edmond. "At this point, I will risk detection. I can't stand being bitten one more time." She then began to climb the steep embankment that led to the road.

The sun was rapidly rising above them. Soon they arrived at a crossroad. The hand-painted sign read STINKY TOE LANE.

"We are in luck. This is the first good thing that has happened to us," said Edmond. "Stinky Toe Lane is mentioned on the map. We can't be too far from the O'Dea house. Perhaps an hour or two more of walking."

As they walked, they became aware of their increasing fatigue. Their adrenaline had given them an artificial sense of endurance. Their feet ached with each step on the unpaved road. Their open cuts continued to attract flies and when they stopped in the shade to rest, mosquitoes approached them in abundant numbers. Finally they came to a small stream that cascaded down the hill.

They both waded into the stream that flowed by the side of the road before vanishing under it on its way to the sea. They drank and washed their hands, arms, legs and every part of their bodies in the cold fast-running water. The waters were covered by the shadows of the rain forest. When they heard a tractor coming down the road, they lowered their bodies further into the water until they were no longer visible from the road. "What if the stream is not safe for drinking?" asked Magdalene as an afterthought.

"At this stage, it is better to stay hydrated and to lower our body temperatures. Whatever we catch as far as bacteria is concerned, we can worry about later."

Soon the engine sounds grew faint as the worker drove away from them.

"Perhaps I should have gone to confession when we were at the church. Obviously I have a lot to ask forgiveness for," said Edmond.

"Why don't I play the role of the priest and you confess your sins to me?" Magdalene laughed.

Edmond did not know how to respond. While joking at times about his past, all traces of humor had now vanished from him. Perhaps his fatigue made him too serious. The more that he was with Magdalene, the less he guarded his emotions. The defenses that defined his personality were slowly breaking away.

After one more hour of continuous walking, they spotted a well-tended eight-foot stone wall with concertina razor wire above it. They approached a gate that was secured by a lock and chain in addition to a deadbolt.

"I have never seen such home security before. I expect to find a moat on the other side of the wall," said Edmond with a smile. "This seems to be the location indicated on the map." Since the gate did not have razor wire above it, they both climbed over the metal gate and began to walk down a winding road that led up a hill. "You may not have noticed it, but there was an infrared beam just above the gate that is designed to send an intruder alarm to the owner. Whoever he is, he doesn't like surprises."

There sitting on top of a hillock was a beautiful multilevel Caribbean-style house. They could see the manicured lawn and the sparkling waters of a large, well-maintained swimming pool.

As they approached the house, two large dogs stood on their haunches and began to bark and growl. It was apparent that the two dogs were awaiting a command before attacking. Edmond and Magdalene did not know what to do. They knew that if the two dogs pursued them, they would never make it back to the gate. Suddenly a small gray-haired man appeared on the porch. In his hand was a double-barreled shotgun.

"What do you two want?" shouted the man.

"Is this the O'Dea house?" Edmond responded.

"Who is asking?"

"My name is Edmond. This is my wife Magdalene."

"Like I said, what do you two want? You are on private land. We do not provide access to the beach. For that you need to continue down the road for another quarter of a mile."

"We would like to talk to you about Ann," replied

Edmond.

"Ann?" he replied.

"Yes, Ann," Edmond shouted. "My wife knew her. They were good friends."

The man on the porch squinted and shielded his eyes from the sun. He then motioned for them to approach the house. With a wave of his hand, the two dogs lay on their bellies, motionless. Even though silent, they followed the two visitors with their eyes.

"I am John, Ann's father," he said as he opened the breech of the shotgun removing two shells. "You can't be too careful when strangers approach. My wife tells me I am overly cautious. In the Caribbean, it is not uncommon for the rich to be harassed."

He led them into a great room with a high wood ceiling from which rotating fans were suspended. A large sailing ship adorned the fireplace mantle. An eclectic collection of photographs rested on the tables of the room. Edmond picked up one and asked, "Is this Ann when she was young?"

"No, afraid not. Just before Ann left for Ireland to pursue her medical degree, we had a terrible fire. The house burned down. We built this one over the same spot. Luckily for us, the garden and pool cabana were untouched. You know, fire can be very selective." He paused. "All photographs of Ann perished in the blaze. The flames shot hundreds of feet into the air. Some say it formed a fire tornado, just like the pillar of fire that guided Moses in the Bible. Of course, the uneducated always exaggerate. That is what makes them such good storytellers.

"The locals said they had never seen anything burn like the house did. I still can't believe that it happened. At first we thought it was an electrical problem, but there's no way of knowing. Unlike in your country, we do not have the ability to find the origin of a fire on our island. Not enough burns here on its own to justify the expense. Of course, Soufriere Hills burned everything in its path." He looked away. "May I get you a drink?"

"Yes," said Edmond, "we would both appreciate a glass of water. If you have any ice, that would make it much better. I think we got overheated on our walk here."

Magdalene asked, "Did your daughter return to setup a practice on Montserrat?"

"No, we are too small an island for her specialty. She trained as an OB/GYN."

Looking at John, Magdalene said, "Perhaps we have the wrong Ann in mind. The Ann that I knew was certainly not a doctor." As she confided in him, Magdalene noticed a recent painting that startled her. "Who is the subject of that painting?"

"It is a painting of Ann from memory. You see, my wife is a very good artist even though she will not admit it to anyone."

"It is a remarkable likeness of her," said Magdalene. "Your wife is truly a gifted artist."

"Please excuse me while I try to locate my wife in the garden. She will want to meet both of you." John O'Dea left the room.

"Edmond, something is very wrong here."

"I imagine Ann told them that she was going to school in Ireland. She did not want to worry them. Of course, it would take a great deal of courage to admit the truth that she had become a hooker," said Edmond.

John returned with his wife who extended her hand first to Magdalene and then to John. "My name is Mary. I understand that both of you knew our daughter. Please tell me how you became acquainted with her."

Edmond looked at Magdalene. "It was my wife that knew her."

"Yes, we were friends in Barbados," said Magdalene.

"I am sorry but my daughter never traveled to Barbados except when we visited there when she was very young. Maybe ten or twelve."

As they talked, Edmond stared at the painting. There was something very familiar to him about it. At first he did not pay attention to it since it was a primitive painting lacking the refinements essential to fine art. Yet it bothered him. The red hair, narrow cheekbones and the intense stare that compelled him to look deeper into her blue eyes. Then it dawned on him, she was the woman in his dream. The guardian of the graves near the castle that he and April had shared.

He thought, "No, it can't be. The painting's lack of refinement just makes Ann look like many other red-haired people that I have seen in Ireland. You see only what you want in a painting. Yet she seems very familiar."

"Edmond, you haven't told us your last name," said John from across the room.

"Sorry, sir. It is Bryant."

"Well Edmond, you and your wife look like you could use a change of clothing and a good bath. You two must have been walking for hours."

"John, that would be very nice of you," replied Magdalene. "We are very tired, and I am afraid that we became more ambitious in our walk than we should have been."

"I want you two to lodge with us for the night. That is unless you have made arrangements elsewhere."

"What a kind offer. We will accept," said Edmond.

Edmond and Magdalene were shown to the guestroom that overlooked the swimming pool and the Caribbean Sea. The clouds were already wearing the colors of approaching twilight.

"Edmond, I have no idea what is going on. I really believe that painting is of the Ann that I have known for almost a year. Why won't they admit that their daughter worked in Barbados?"

"Magdalene, be careful of what you say or ask. Based on the security system around the house, I would speculate that these rooms have electronic ears. When something is confidential, write it down."

As he undressed, Edmond did not reply to her previous question regarding the parents. They both entered the large bath that reminded him of the hot sea baths he had taken in Yokosuka. They were both too exhausted to be aware of each other's nudity. Edmond rested his head against the tile and closed his eyes. Soon he was asleep in the hot circulating water.

In his dream, he was walking along a black-sand beach. In the distance he could see a beautiful young woman approaching him. Her hair was colored by the sunset. Then as she neared, she extended her hands as if to embrace him. His heart beat loudly in his ears. It was April.

Then her face changed gradually as though it were an image in a kaleidoscope. The woman that he had loved metamorphosed into that of Ann. She appeared to be walking above the waters of the River Lee. The air was cold with falling mist. Her white gown flowed behind her as she approached him like a fog hovering above the surface of the rapidly flowing water.

Suddenly he was struggling to surface from the river. He had fallen down a steep embankment into its flowing current while mesmerized by the image before him. In the clear frigid water, he could see the reeds that adorned the bank. He struggled to regain the rock ledge from which he had just fallen but it was futile. The more he tried, the further the distance increased. Looking up, he saw her through the clear, freezing water.

She bent down to take his hand. At the touch, she was suddenly standing among the Celtic crosses that adorned the rural cemetery. It was she, the Ann that he had seen in the graveyard in the woods near the castle. The graveyard that April could not locate as they drove searching for it.

"Edmond, wake up!" Magdalene said, shaking him. "You were talking in your sleep. I have never known a man to fall asleep so quickly. You were calling Ann just before I awoke you. Do you know another Ann?"

Edmond raised himself from the warm water of the swirling bath. "I am sorry. I think that my lack of sleep has caught up with me."

Mary had brought them bathrobes. It was apparent that she was washing their soiled clothing. Edmond looked at Magdalene as she first shook and then squeezed the water from her long red hair.

Magdalene looked down at him. "I don't know what to say to them. If I tell them the truth about Ann, they will ask us to leave. It is apparent that they do not know what really happened to her."

Edmond said, "You are positive that the Ann in the painting is the one you know? Remember, it is a primitive painting composed from memory."

Magdalene replied, "I am absolutely certain. That is the woman, my friend, who worked at the brothel with me. You may not have noticed but the plaque at the bottom of the painting read ANN PENNINGTON."

"Ann Pennington? I thought O'Dea was her last name!"

"No. She liked to use her middle name as her last name."

"Why didn't you tell me this before?"

"I should have but I did not trust you then."

"I wish I could have met her. The painting of her is very beautiful," said Edmond. He did not want to remind her again that he had been looking for a person with that same name, a person who was no longer alive. Now he knew that the only real Ann Pennington was dead.

Edmond needed time to reason out what was happening. Nothing that had occurred was logical to him.

After dressing, they joined John and Mary on the porch facing the Caribbean Sea. Edmond addressed them both, "I envy Ann growing up in such a beautiful and serene place. Both of my parents were teachers. As a result, I never experienced this type of luxury." After a pause, Edmond continued, "Please forgive me for being so inquisitive. If I remember correctly, she was sent to a parochial school in Ireland. After graduating, she attended medical school in that country. I assume that she is now practicing there?"

"Yes, of course," replied Mary.

Edmond sensed that something was not right in her story about her daughter's life. The package was too neat. A beautiful woman who could tempt any man lived a perfect life. He felt that there must be a lot that they were not telling or that they do not want Edmond and Magdalene to know.

Edmond observed the eyes of John as Mary talked. He appeared very impatient with the conversation. The more Edmond and Magdalene questioned them, the more uneasy he appeared.

The evening arrived quickly and with it the tropical darkness. In the distance they could see the glowing dome of the volcano. Its breath could be faintly smelled in the light trade winds. The frogs croaked loudly in the rain forest, drowning out the songs of the night birds.

After sitting on the veranda, Edmond rose. "John, Mary, thank you for such a delightful meal, the bath and lodgings that you have provide to us. Your kindness to strangers will always be remembered. With your approval, Magdalene and I would like to retire to our bed. I hope you don't object, but I am an early riser. I would like to go for a swim in the sea near sunrise."

John responded, "No problem at all. We will see you in the morning. Coffee and tea will be served on the veranda around ten o'clock."

Edmond and Magdalene went to their room. After undressing, Edmond stood before the open window, looking at the moon-painted sea below the villa. "We are missing something. I don't feel comfortable in continuing to ask them where Ann is now. What a foolish question. We both know the answer. Did they ever find the body?"

"They located her body at sea about two weeks after she had vanished. I am certain that they had some difficulty in identifying her. I think they felt confident that it was Ann only because of her clothing, small size and red hair."

"Where was the funeral held?" asked Edmond.

"At a Catholic church in Saint James. I think that it was St. Mark's," responded Magdalene.

"Her parents were not at the funeral?"

"No, I don't remember them being there. It was a brief Catholic ceremony. More of a church thing than a remembrance of her. I don't think the priest knew what to say about Ann."

"Who attended?"

"The madam of the house and myself. We were the only ones present."

"Weren't the police curious regarding why she got caught in the net of an international fishing boat?" asked Edmond.

"Remember, she was a prostitute without a family as far as we knew at the time."

"What about her uncle and other relatives living in Barbados?"

Magdalene responded quietly, "I feel like she created a family that did not exist. Her 'uncle' was a man who frequented the whorehouse. I think he started to care for her after a while.

She was a person that was easy to love.

"He was the only person that she felt she could trust other than me. As I mentioned before, she did not confide in me totally or really trust me with all of her secrets. Whoever is trying to kill us must think she told me everything, but that is not true."

"I am sorry for repeating the same questions over and over, but I want to make sense of what is happening."

The frogs continued to make their unnatural sounds until suddenly they became silent. Edmond and Magdalene looked at one another. In the quiet of the moment, they could hear John and Mary talking. It sounded like they were arguing loudly yet their words were indistinct. Finally they heard Mary crying. An interior door slammed shut.

Edmond continued to look at the sea. Below, the foam of breakers glistened in the moonlight. Far away, the large swells breaking upon the reef could be seen. In the dim light of night, an object suddenly appeared: faint, distant, vapor like in its appearance. Edmond sensed that there was someone standing under a large breadfruit tree watching him, waiting for him.

He touched Magdalene's shoulder. "Do you see it?"

"See what?" she replied.

"Over there under the tree!"

"I am sorry but I do not see anything. If you see something or someone, it is probably one of the owner's donkeys. With the moon out, they graze in the moonlight."

"No, I am telling you that it was a person or at least I think it was." Edmond paused for a moment. "I have to admit I do not see anything now. Perhaps it was my imagination."

As they stood close to one another, adorned only by

moonlight, Edmond took her hand and held it lightly.

"Do you want me?" she asked almost apologetically.

"I am too haunted by images to love again."

Magdalene squeezed his hand tightly. "I also know that the past is too frequently the present. I have never been loved, but I can imagine what it must be like. To be needed and cared for," Magdalene said, looking up at him.

The morning came almost immediately. They were awakened by the patterns of sunlight as light passed through the shutters. Edmond awoke first. He lay on his side looking at the beauty of the woman beside him. She appeared too fragile to have lived, however briefly, her former life. He noticed the shape of her mouth, the ease with which she breathed. He looked at the outline of her body still covered by the sheet. She awoke as he stared.

"I could feel you looking at me," she said with a soft smile. "I hope you did not mind awakening next to me. I love you being so close. I feel so safe with you near me. Tonight if you do not mind, please hold me in your arms. No man has ever cared enough to do that."

"If we are still here, I will hold you," said Edmond. "Please do not think I am rejecting you as a woman. There is just so much that consumes my thoughts. The more I think about it, the image that I saw under the tree last night must have been purely a product of my imagination. It is only my longing that wants it to be true. If this were Ireland, I would think that the fairies were playing with me."

"Well, it is a kind of Ireland." She laughed. "I thought

that fairies were always good."

"No, I am afraid not. The Irish prefer to keep their distance from them. The tricks they play are often malicious."

As they lay together, everything within him desired her. He wanted to hold her, embrace her and to become a part of her body, yet he knew that their lives could end at any moment and that there was no time for either love or affection. The overwhelming desire within him was simply for them to live.

They walked softly into the dining room where a young island girl was preparing breakfast. "Good morning," he said with a smile. "My name is Edmond and my wife's name is Magdalene."

"Hello, sir," she responded in acknowledgement of his presence. "My name is Elizabeth." She quickly returned to her function of placing napkins and breakfast rolls on the table.

The smell of freshly made coffee floated throughout the dining room as well as the pungent scent of bread.

"Have you known the family long?" Edmond asked.

"You mean the O'Dea family? Yes, for five years."

"Did you ever meet Ann?"

"Oh yes sir. She is a very pretty girl. She has the reddest hair you will ever see."

"What kind of a person is she?" asked Magdalene, hoping to confirm whether or not this Ann was her friend.

"She is very nice to me. She treats me as her equal whenever she visits."

"I understand she lives in Ireland."

"I don't know. No one ever told me where she is living. I did read the travel tag on her luggage. It said Barbados."

"Why would she go to Barbados if she is living in Ireland?" asked Edmond.

"I don't know. You will have to ask Mr. O'Dea that question."

Standing in the entryway to the dining room was Ann's father. He wore a light cotton white shirt and khaki pants. "I happened to overhear your conversation with Elizabeth. I would prefer that you ask either me or my wife about Ann. I think we are in a better position to know her than our hired help."

"Certainly, sir," responded Edmond as though speaking to a superior officer.

"Breakfast was her favorite meal. She would tell Elizabeth exactly what she wanted to have the night before."

Magdalene, who was standing nearby, knew that the Ann she had grown to like never ate breakfast. Like most of the women in the brothel, she would sleep past noon.

Edmond looked at John. "I mentioned yesterday evening that I would enjoy a swim in the sea. I noticed that there is a walkway down to the beach. I am afraid that I have missed my morning swim. May I go for a dip in the late afternoon?"

"Why would you want to get in salt water when we have a very nice freshwater pool right here at the house?"

Edmond responded, "I enjoy the freedom that the sea provides. The bottom must be littered with interesting and unusual shells that I have never seen before. The sea here must also be filled with tropical fish that I have only seen in aquariums."

"I suggest that you return before dark. Sharks like to

feed in darkness." He paused for a moment. "Even though we are safe here at the compound, I cannot guarantee your safety on the beach. If someone approaches you, just tell them that you are a guest of the O'Dea family. The locals all know us so there should not be a problem."

Edmond said, "I know you are safe here, but why the extra precautions such as the dogs and a gun?"

"We occasionally have some less than desirable people arrive on the island. They usually come to sell drugs. As you know, we have several other islands nearby where dealers distribute drugs."

"We have not heard the news in a few days. Anything of interest happening in the Caribbean?" asked Edmond.

"Just the arrival and departure in Antigua of some of the world's largest and most expensive yachts. It is funny how people like to read about what they will never have." He paused. "I read that an abandoned vessel was found two hundred or so nautical miles from here. It was sailing just fine until the inter-island marine patrol attempted to stop it for possible drug running. When they boarded it, they found no trace of the crew. Things like that do happen."

"A shame for the crew," Edmond said, glancing at Magdalene.

Mary entered the room and sat down. "Magdalene, please tell me more about how you know Ann. We would love to know more about how she is doing."

Magdalene paused for a moment. "She was doing fine the last time I saw here. Just fine. She loves to tell stories about her home here on Montserrat. She mentioned how wonderful you two were when she was growing up. I know she misses you very much."

"How is her practice going? Did she say if she had many patients?"

"If I remember correctly, she said that she had more patients than she could attend to. Of course, she was only kidding. You know how she loves to exaggerate." Magdalene looked once more at the painting. "That is such a realistic painting of her. She appears so very happy as she gazes upon the sea beyond the cliff. She often mentioned how she loved the ocean. I don't think she was ever afraid of it, not even during hurricane season."

"Hurricane season?" questioned Mary.

"She talked about the great hurricane that destroyed so much of your island many years ago. That was when she mentioned that she did not fear the great storms.

John said, "Of course we do not like to think about hurricanes. In 1986, Hurricane Hugo destroyed or damaged more than half of the buildings on the island. We were not living here at the time. But we heard many stories about what occurred. As you might have guessed, we live in a fool's paradise."

Edmond did not know how to respond to John. It was possible that he was joking about the island's misfortune and perhaps even about himself.

John glanced at Edmond. "I hope you two will excuse us. Mary and I must do our weekly shopping in Brades. I sometimes send Elizabeth but she always buys too much. There are only the two of us to feed. But you know what, since you are here, we'll get lobsters and treat you to a real island feast. Yes, indeed we should."

"Mr. O'Dea, if you don't mind, please do not call attention to our being here. You have spoiled us enough. I am afraid that our presence already raises the curiosity of strangers. Honeymooners need and love their privacy," Edmond said with a smile.

"Edmond, I have no intention of mentioning you or Magdalene's presence as our guests. We all need our private moments, especially when we are in love. Besides, our neighbors already view us with suspicion. We know how the poor feel about those who have more than they especially on a small island such as this."

John paused. "I am afraid that Elizabeth will not be here to serve you since she always goes home early in the evening. Her house is located about a mile or so down the coast road from here. Please make yourself at home while we are away shopping."

Magdalene and Edmond watched as the O'Dea's Mini Cooper left the driveway. Edmond whispered to Magdalene, "This is our chance to see if we can find out more about Ann. I noticed that John has an office just down the hall from our room. I don't want to go through their drawers, but let's look for any photographs that might assist us. They said that the house burned down and everything was lost, but I am not so sure I believe that story."

They walked down the wide hall to the library and office. The walls and ceilings were of Honduran mahogany. Edmond had never seen such expensive wood used so abundantly for entire walls. As he looked about, he realized that Ann's parents were living a life of great abundance.

"Magdalene, I am beginning to wonder if these are really her parents. Is it possible that she was referring to them as surrogates or perhaps even as her employers? Perhaps they were offering her the security and accountability that she had never known from her real parents. It is difficult for me to judge the relationship between Mary and John."

"You are wrong. She had no need to lie to me. Ann often described their love for her. She mentioned that they gave her anything she wanted. I was very jealous of the jewelry and clothing that they gave her. Ann lacked for nothing."

"If that is the case, why did she become a prostitute? I understand that you felt you had little or no alternatives but Ann . . . she could have had anything she wanted."

"There is a simple answer: Heroin! She was very much addicted to it. Ann did not want to worry or offend her parents. She fell in love with a member of the cartel. He was the one who introduced her to the drug and then later abandoned her. There was no way that she could support her habit except in the brothel."

"Her parents could have provided whatever treatment was necessary. Why didn't she ask them for help?"

Magdalene thought for a moment. "Perhaps she did not want to worry them. As you may know, a heroin addict remains a slave to the drug for life. Intervention does not prevent relapse."

Edmond looked at her. "How did you avoid addiction?"

"I've seen too many people like Ann. I did not want to wake up and see myself as a ghost in a mirror," she answered. "I always hoped that one fine day someone would rescue me, and that I could find some degree of happiness. Perhaps my being so naïve provided me with the will to resist."

They scanned the walls in the other rooms. Regardless of their previous intention, they looked carefully in the drawers of the office desk but could find no information to help them solve the mystery of her death. "I can't believe that primitive painting is the only trace of their daughter," said Edmond. "More should remain of a person, especially a daughter. Some items such as dolls or pictures. Even if the fire destroyed the house completely, there are always relics left behind."

Three o'clock arrived and then four. "I think it is time for me to go for a swim. Would you like to join me?" asked Edmond.

"No, I will lounge about until you return," said Magdalene. "I want to take advantage of their wealth while I can. I have never been so comfortable in my life. I can't imagine that families get to live like this."

Edmond walked down the steep path that led past a coconut grove to where the Caribbean touched the black sands of the beach. The sand possessed an unending variety of sparkling colors. It glistened when touched by the waters of the sea.

As he entered the water, the warmth of the salt water felt very good to his tired legs. The strong breeze chased the heat ashore. He turned and swam on his back while gazing up at the tall anvil shaped clouds that were congregating about the hilltops of the island. He knew that rain would soon be falling, a soft perfumed rain followed by a rainbow.

Then, at an angle to him, he saw a woman swimming with her head barely above the water. He turned over and began a slow rhythmic breaststroke. He swam slowly in order to render himself just above the surface of the water while barely kicking his feet. Edmond could not tell if the woman had seen him or not.

He watched as she reached the shore, alone and naked in radiant beauty, her skin the color of abalone shell. Her red hair caught the rays of the late afternoon sun as light sparkled off her back. She did not turn towards him as he watched. Instead she entered into the edge of the rain forest and vanished.

Edmond quickly swam to where she had last appeared, free of the breakers that fell upon the volcanic rocks that stood as sentinels to the beach. He followed her footprints past the coconut trees to a freshwater stream that descended from the rain forest. At the base of the stream was a waterfall whose clear water cascaded into a small pool in which she now swam, freeing the salt and sand from her body.

Edmond approached her, careful to make enough noise to alert her to his presence. "I could not help but notice you swimming in the Caribbean. At first I did not know what to think. A beautiful woman cast from the sea, of such happenings legends are made."

Upon seeing Edmond, she bade him to enter the pool of cool water. At first she just glanced at him, then a smile came on her face. "You must be the friend of Magdalene's that I have heard the villagers talking about."

"Perhaps I am that person, but who are you and how do you know my relationship with Magdalene?" Edmond asked.

"Elizabeth told me about you and my friend Magdalene.

She said that you had just arrived on the island. You did not know it, but she took a picture of you with her iPhone. I knew it was you when you first entered the sea."

"Well, you know more about me than I know about you. Please tell me your name."

"My name is Ann Pennington," she responded.

"No, it is not. Ann Pennington O'Dea is in Ireland. The Ann that Magdalene knew is dead. Be honest with me and tell me who you are," he said in a demanding tone.

She did not respond but began to swim towards the center of the pool of cool, fresh water. She turned and faced him in silence.

"If you are Ann Pennington, why did you not make your presence known to us earlier?" he asked.

"We are all in danger," she said quietly, looking about the vines and trees that hovered near the waters of the pool.

"I know that Magdalene and I are in harm's way, but why are you?"

"You have not figured it out yet?" she asked.

"Figured what out? And by the way, what is your real name?"

"Like I told you, I am Ann Pennington."

"That I cannot believe regardless of how many times you tell me. We both know that Ann died in Barbados several weeks ago. For some reason the people that killed her want to harm us, too. We came to Montserrat since Ann's parents might be able to help hide us."

"My parents?" Ann laughed.

"Yes, they are her parents. Magdalene said that Ann mentioned them frequently."

"When I first came to Barbados from Venezuela, I was fleeing from an unhappy relationship with a young lover. I had no money or anything of value. That was when I met John O'Dea in Barbados. Even though he was much older, he impressed me with his wealth and caring attitude. We had a brief affair on the island. He then took me to Montserrat and introduced me to his wife. I don't know if she ever knew that we had been lovers.

"They were so nice to me that I soon referred to them as Mom and Papa. The O'Deas were the ones who took me back to Barbados to work in the brothel. You see, they own it. They are involved in many unlawful businesses including drug trafficking throughout the Caribbean and Europe." She paused. "I never realized Magdalene would take it literally when I called them Mom and Papa."

"Since you are alive, whose body was found in the ocean?"

"A young woman died in my place. She was my friend. She didn't even work in the brothel but instead in a local gift shop. I gave her some of my clothes and even the belt with my name engraved in the leather. The killers mistook her for me because of the purse she was carrying. It had my initials on it. It was through the belt, however, that the police identified her body as mine."

"Why are you here if the O'Dea family is so dangerous?"

"I did not know at the time what they were capable of. When the body was discovered by a fisherman, I knew my life was in danger. I was staying with a man that I met on the beach. I was with him when I heard the news that Ann Pennington's body had been discovered at sea. Of course, I did not mention who I really was to him. At the time, I did not realize that the O'Deas were the ones that wanted me dead. I didn't know who was trying to kill me. That is why I came to Montserrat. I thought they would protect me."

"Why didn't they kill you when you first arrived at the house?"

"They are not killers. It is too messy and needs to be left to the professionals. Besides, I was friends with Elizabeth. If they murder me, they would have to kill her and her father as well. They are just stalling until their hitman arrives from Jamaica to do the job correctly."

"Once in Montserrat who told you that they were going to murder you?" asked Edmond.

"Elizabeth heard James talking on his satellite phone. She warned me. The moment I knew the truth I ran to Elizabeth's house and have hidden there ever since. Of course, they know I am there. It is just a matter of time until they come for me." She paused and then continued, "I was hoping to find you and Magdalene before you were both dead. I was bathing in the ocean when you saw me."

"Why didn't you go to the police when you arrived in Montserrat?"

"Would they have believed a dead girl?" she replied, laughing uneasily.

"You didn't send me any messages on Facebook, did you?" asked Edmond.

"No, of course not. I don't even know who you are except that you are Magdalene's friend."

"I have been looking for Ann Pennington ever since someone by that name posted messages on my Facebook page."

"There are many Ann Penningtons. My father named me after an early actress that he thought was very beautiful. She too had red hair and was small like me." She paused and then looked into his eyes. "We need to flee Montserrat as soon as we can. Is Magdalene at the O'Dea house?"

"Yes, she is there now."

They quickly left the pool of water, dressed in what they had brought to the beach and then sprinted up the steep path towards the house. Upon arriving at the estate, Edmond shouted, "Magdalene! Magdalene!" There was no reply. He ran from room to room looking for her. Then he saw her in the garden surrounded by the two large Irish wolfhounds who appeared to be guarding her. She was stroking their thick fur as their tails wagged in approval. They growled at Edmond's approach.

"Ann, what on earth?" Magdalene shouted as she ran towards her. "You are dead! You are supposed to be dead!"

"Magdalene, we have to flee as quickly as possible. I will explain later what happened. I am so sorry you got involved in all of this. I never wanted you in harm's way. Help me gather food and anything else we might need to survive on the island. Look for guns, a bow and arrow, flashlights, medical kits, anything that we can carry. There are some large cloth bags in the utility room that we can use to pack the items in. I thought that they would not kill me if I stayed out of the way, but with your arrival all that has changed."

"Where can we hide?" asked Edmond. "The villagers will see us and tell John O'Dea. There is no way they could know that they are pursuing us. For all we know, the assassins have already arrived on the island."

Ann replied, "The only place that we can go where they will not look for us is in the exclusion zone. Perhaps I should have gone there earlier, but there may not be any food or water. Besides, I could not have carried supplies to last more than three or four days. It is really too dangerous for anyone to enter alone but we have no choice. Elizabeth's father has a hut on a small hill surrounded by but not covered in lava. He still goes there when the moon is full to tend his garden. He loves it there since that was where he was born and brought up. He will not leave it. So far the security forces have not arrested him. Since everyone has been warned, they see little reason to search the area for local intruders. The exclusion zone, as you know, is nearly two-thirds of Montserrat. I am sure they feel that if someone is crazy enough to enter the forbidden area, then they do not need to be saved."

As Ann searched for needed items, she continued, "There are goats and Blackbelly sheep living there. We will have enough meat and vegetables from the garden to live on until we can escape. I do not know where to go or how to escape, but eventually we must get off Montserrat. We have to be careful. Elizabeth told me that the volcanologists are telling the locals to be prepared to evacuate at a moment's notice. The volcano is showing signs of a possible eruption."

"Ann, I am not so sure about entering the exclusion zone," said Edmond. "When we saw the mountain by moonlight, it appeared to very violent. We too had previously heard some people saying that they expected an eruption at any time. The new eruption is expected to be more violent than the one that destroyed the capital. If it is more destructive, your little hill that was spared the first time might not be so fortunate next time."

Ann replied, "Regardless of the risk, we need to leave this house before they return. I have already spoken to Elizabeth and asked her father's permission for us to use the cottage."

"Why will Elizabeth and her father not join us? I would think that they are in as much danger as we are. When we are found missing, John will make the connection instantly."

"Elizabeth's father is an invalid now that he has broken his hip. There is no way that he can make the journey. He cannot even stand without her help. She will have to stay and take care of him. Elizabeth did make one request – she said to remove the black stone in the garden wall. It is already loose and should be easy to slide out."

"Why does she want us to do that?" asked Magdalene.

"Elizabeth said that her father had placed some family heirlooms in an old leather medical case. If the volcano erupts again, he is afraid that the case will be buried in the lava. It has a small padlock on it, and he asked that we not remove the lock until we return it to Elizabeth."

"That is a small favor to ask in exchange for the use of his cottage," replied Edmond who was busy collecting the necessary items to take with them. He hesitated. "Will we not be seen entering the forbidden zone in daylight?"

"We will not enter until the moon rises tonight. There will then be enough light for us to make the journey. That is why it is important for us to find flashlights. The flashlights should have red filters with them. Just be sure you place it over the lens when you cut the light on so as to reduce the likelihood of the beam being seen." Ann paused. "We will wait in the rain forest until dark."

They each carried items necessary for their journey. They knew that as soon as John returned, the search for them would begin. The only weapon that was not locked in the armory was a crossbow with three arrows.

As they walked across the yard, the Irish wolfhounds began to growl and bark. Edmond said, "Fortunately you made friends with them in the garden. Nonetheless, I am glad you locked the garden gate behind you."

"Let's pray that the breed is not very good at tracking," said Ann.

"On this small island, we are out of luck if they are," said Edmond as they entered the thick undergrowth.

Soon they were walking in a streambed where the fresh water felt cool to their feet and legs. "Let's walk in the stream as far as we can to make it more difficult for the dogs to track us," said Edmond.

After leaving the stream, they climbed high enough to encounter the first signs of molten rock. In the shade of a large ledge of frozen lava, they stopped and waited for the rising moon. The sparkling Caribbean, adorned in beautiful clouds that fled from the southern edge of the ocean, lay before them. The coolness of the shade and rock, as well as the constant wind, made their waiting almost comfortable.

As they looked south, they could see the smoke from the volcano streaming out over the ocean. The brownish black smoke drifted not only over the sea but rose in a towering column into the sky. While seated on the ledge, they could feel the trembling of the mountain beneath them. It was as though the earth was experiencing spasms of cataclysmic proportions.

Edmond stood up and climbed to the top of the ledge and looked towards where the capital had been before the eruption. He could see the decaying walls and rusted remnants of the roofs of the few structures that could still be identified as businesses. The small wooden houses of the capital had burned before being buried in the lava that flowed down the slopes of the volcano.

He looked down at the two women. "I have never seen anything like this before. I cannot imagine having been in the capital when the eruption occurred. What terror the residents must have felt."

Magdalene looked up at him and smiled. "At least we are alive. I don't think they will follow us here. At least I hope not. I am beginning, however, to think that this might not have been such a good idea. We are too close to the volcano."

The moon appeared as the evening star became more brilliant in the west. The moon changed its color from deep red to warm orange as it rose higher. Soon Artemis appeared as a silver disk. As it continued its ascent in the night sky, Edmond, Ann and Magdalene began to walk towards the refuge on the hill that until now had been but a drawing on a map.

"Had it not been for Elizabeth, we would have no hope at all," said Magdalene, carefully placing her feet on the ground to avoid slipping.

As they climbed, they grew closer to the Soufriere Hills

volcano. Its fiery glow illuminated the night sky like that of Vulcan's forge. The ground moved as small earthquakes shook their steps.

They walked ever higher on the outskirts of Plymouth. The former city was silent in the night as moonlight reflected off the remains of what few structures had survived the onslaught. "Like Magdalene," said Edmond, "I am not so sure this was a wise decision. Now that we are closer to the volcano, it seems more violent than I could have ever imagined. I am surprised that they have not yet evacuated the entire island. I have a strong feeling that another eruption is going to occur shortly." Suddenly, he pointed to a steam vent not far from their trail. "Over there, look! I swear that plume of steam was not there before."

"Edmond, what choice do we have but to go on?" Ann asked as she studied the map illuminated by the red glow of her flashlight. "The hill is just a short distance from us according to the sketch that Elizabeth gave me. It is only good luck that the cottage survived the collapse of the dome and the pyroclastic flow that followed. It is like one of those freak accidents wherein everyone on the airplane is killed but one person."

Just as despair set in, grass and small trees appeared before them. It was like an island surrounded by a sea of frozen lava. "I can't believe that the heat and ash didn't kill everything here now, even the seeds," said Edmond as they continued their climb.

Suddenly before them was a cottage made of cinder block with a metal roof. There were no doors or windows. Just the shell of a house. It was gray in color like the landscape around it, illuminated only by twilight.

Edmond walked into the cottage as the sun's first rays fell upon the mountains of Montserrat. The cottage walls, at one time, must have been painted a light lime green. The ceiling, that had once been yellow, now appeared gray from the ash clinging tenaciously to it. The unmade bed was covered in ashes as were the two chairs and dining table. Edmond looked behind him and saw the imprints of his steps in the volcanic ash. He realized how easy it would be to track their movements.

Ann and Magdalene entered the house and stood without saying a word as they surveyed the uninhabitable dwelling. "Edmond, look out the window! There's a goat grazing on some green grass. You can shoot it with your crossbow. At least we can have some meat," said Ann enthusiastically.

Edmond responded, "Everything is covered in ash. I don't even know if we have anything to cook it in. If we plan to remain here, the most important thing we need to find is water. Did you see a well?"

Ann replied, "Yes, there is one under the charred breadfruit tree. Let's hope the water is still good. There is a catchment tank at the back of the house but any rainwater collected off the roof will be undrinkable. Our Garden of Eden may simply be but a variation of hell."

Edmond walked outside to the well. After drawing up a bucket, the water appeared black. "This water is undrinkable," he shouted. "Wait, I hear moving water like that coming from a stream." Edmond made his way through the young trees and there before him was a flowing stream, clear and cool to the touch. "At least there is enough water for bathing and cleaning the house. I will taste it to see if it is okay to drink." With those words, he bent down to his knees and cupped the cool water in his hands. Even though it smelled of sulfur, he felt that it was safe enough to drink.

By afternoon, they had cleaned the house enough to make it suitable as a temporary dwelling. Later, Edmond killed the goat that Ann had spotted. By evening it was roasting on a fire that Edmond had built where the lava flow was high enough to prevent the firelight from being seen in the late twilight. The smoke would not generate any interest since steam vents were active below them.

As the sun neared the sea, they bathed in the clear waters of the stream. Edmond knew that they were as marooned as Robinson Crusoe had been. Instead of an uncharted sea before them, there were the gray deposits of pyroclastic and volcanic mudflows. Beyond the desolation that was before them lay almost certain death at the hands of assassins.

Edmond could still not figure out why they were being pursued. What made the deaths of Ann and Magdalene and now his own of such importance? What could Ann have discovered that was so significant?

That evening as Ann and Magdalene lay on the only bed, Edmond remained awake sitting in a cane chair. He looked upon the two beautiful women who slept so soundly not with lust but with overwhelming sadness. He also thought of April whom he still loved.

In the very early morning hours, the sound of a tremendous explosion occurred. "Wake up!" shouted Edmond. "The last explosion that we heard may be a precursor to a major dome collapse. If so, we may not make it back down the mountain. Pyroclastic flows can seal off any escape route. Let's pray the volcano will pause long enough for us to flee with our lives." As he spoke, the ground began to move. Dishes from the cupboard rocked and then fell to the floor below. Birds roosting in the nearby burned forest took to wing, screaming their calls.

Edmond ran outside and climbed to the top of the hill to get a clear and unobstructed view of the volcano. Molten lava was being catapulted into the sky. It seemed like Thor was stirring the great furnace within the mountain. The ground shook with earthquakes.

He ran back down the steep hill towards the cottage. As he ran, he fell. Regaining his stance, he shouted to warn them of the impending eruption. After relating what he had seen, the three remained outside the cottage, each staring at the red glowing furnace that had suddenly become quieter in the early morning twilight as both Venus and Mars neared the horizon of the sea.

"Ann, didn't you say that Elizabeth wanted you to collect a leather satchel from the garden wall? We have to retrieve it quickly. There is no time to delay. What on earth could be in the satchel that makes it so important to Elizabeth's father?"

"She didn't give any specifics. She just said that it probably contained some photographs of her mother and a few family mementos. There could not be anything of value. He tended goats and fished. I doubt if they had anything more than a few East Caribbean dollars. Everything becomes of sentimental value when you're old."

"Let's get the satchel now so we can honor his request –

just in case we have to leave quickly. We can carry it since we will probably have to leave behind everything that we brought here."

"Where did Elizabeth say it was?"

"Behind a black stone in the garden wall," said Ann.

They walked out to the garden area. All of the plants were dead, victims of a layer of ash that had fallen. All the stones in the garden were covered in identical ash.

"We need to wipe the stones with a wet rag to see which one is black. The small stream will give us the needed water."

They then began to wipe the faces of the stones with some discarded rags that they had found in the kitchen. Finally Ann shouted, "Here it is. This stone is darker than the others."

Edmond walked over to Ann and finished washing the stone. It was indeed darker than the rest. At first he tried to dislodge it with his fingers but it would not move. He returned to the cabin and looked for a piece of metal to use. He found a box that contained an ax. With that instrument he began to pry it loose.

After much effort, the stone began to move. Finally it dropped to the ground. There, in front of them, was a decaying satchel. As he lifted it out, he could not believe how heavy it was. There was obviously more in it than papers. Like Elizabeth had previously mentioned, the satchel bore a padlock.

"At least we can keep our word to her father that we got the satchel for him," said Edmond now short of breath. "We owe them that."

Ann looked at him. "When we can, we will take the satchel to Elizabeth. I just hope that will be soon." After she finished speaking, she looked at the volcano that now began to spew forth molten rocks and plumes of steam. The earth moved violently beneath their feet.

Edmond looked at the volcano, then turned his attention towards Plymouth. The desolate city appeared like the bones of a dead animal. What structures remained appeared as sentinels above the frozen lava.

As he stared, he noticed some movement in the city. The brief movement suddenly stopped. They were too far away to make out details. He continued to look in the direction of the buried capital but did not see anything except the buildings frozen in volcanic stone.

"I thought I saw something moving there. It must be a hallucination since I don't see anything now. I just wish I had some field glasses. They would really be a big help now."

Ann and Magdalene turned from looking at the satchel and glanced in the direction of Plymouth. "I don't see anything unusual. Why don't we open the satchel? Maybe it has a pair of binoculars," said Magdalene.

"We can't," responded Ann. "I promised Elizabeth we would not attempt to open it. I told her we would return it as soon as we deemed it safe.

"Well, I imagine that it is simply some old photographs and papers. As a man grows older, he values his memories more than gold. They are the only things that cannot be stolen from him," said Edmond.

Even though the volcano was still emitting steam and smoke, the violent motion of the earth had stopped. Only a small trembling remained. It was as though the mountain needed to rest from its ill-tempered fit.

Ann looked at Edmond. "Maybe a major eruption is not going to occur. I am starving. A meal of protein doesn't last very long especially when it is one of wild goat. We will need food in order to travel down the mountain. There is no way of knowing when we can eat again."

"Well, hunter," said Magdalene, "your task is to bring down another goat for us to cook. Remember that you missed the first time losing the arrow. That cost us one of our arrows. Luckily you brought down that goat with the second one. You could have just as easily walked over and stabbed it with your pocketknife. Have you ever used a crossbow before?"

"Maybe in another life when I was scaling a castle wall in Ireland." Edmond laughed.

Ann laughed back. "Be careful and don't shoot one of us or yourself."

Edmond picked up the crossbow and the remaining arrow and began to scout for a domestic goat who found freedom after the inhabitants fled Plymouth. He climbed higher and higher in his pursuit, being careful not to get spotted by the police should they scan the area for intruders in the exclusion zone.

As he gained a new ridge, he spotted a goat just a few yards away. The animal paused just long enough for Edmond to aim and fire his single arrow. It struck the hindquarter of the animal. It was necessary for Edmond to slit its throat in order to quiet its pain.

He sat down on the rock, shaking for he had never killed anything at such close range. His hands were dripping with blood, his clothing soiled. He hoisted the large animal on his shoulder and began his descend towards the cabin. In the far distance he noticed what appeared to be six or seven men walking through Plymouth. At times, a man would enter an abandoned building and then reemerged to look inside another.

Edmond threw the carcass of the goat down and began to slide down the rocks as quickly as he could towards the cabin. Just as he neared the entrance, a violent explosion occurred on the mountain. Rocks cascaded down its slopes. Ash rose as did a plume of steam. Edmond knew that it was only a short time before the volcano dome would collapse anew, sending lava flowing down the sides of the mountain proceeded by a blast of hot wind and rock that would kill everything in its path.

Panting, he entered the cinder-block cottage. Ann and Magdalene were hugging each other in a corner of the one-room structure. "Quick, grab anything you want to save. We have got to get to the beach as quickly as possible. The volcano is getting ready to erupt anew. My instincts tell me that this time it will utterly destroy the island. Don't carry anything you do not need."

Magdalene did not take anything. Ann grabbed the leather satchel. Edmond carried a climbing rope that he had found in the storage closet of the O'Dea house.

They ran down the hill directly towards the sea. Suddenly earthquakes began to open up the earth in front of them, causing landslides. They managed to leap to safety just as the hill above them rippled.

"Jump! Jump!" shouted Edmond who had spotted a large rock shelf before them. Resting on the shelf was a large formation of hardened lava that could shield them from the gathering avalanche.

Magdalene and Edmond reached the stone shelf and

rolled behind the large lava shield. Ann, who was just behind them, was struck by a large rock. She staggered forward and fell at their feet. Edmond pulled her body behind the shield of hardened lava. Her blood dampened the gray ash that now covered them. He knew she was dead. Magdalene screamed and collapsed into sobs. For some reason unknown even to Edmond, he grabbed the satchel and pushed Magdalene further down the slope.

The land before the sea was level, allowing them to run as fast as they could towards the cliff that dropped precipitously into the Caribbean. When they reached the precipice, they paused. "On the count of three, leap!" shouted Edmond. "One, two, three!" Holding hands, they lunged into the air. He had practiced jumps in order to qualify for commissioning yet he had never leaped from so high a platform before.

Fortunately they landed legs bent, feet first and found themselves bouncing off the coral bottom. Quickly they regained the surface. Edmond had managed to hold onto the satchel by twisting his arm through the straps. When he landed in the water, the satchel almost separated his shoulder. "Swim, swim as fast as you can seaward!" he shouted to Magdalene.

He knew that soon rocks, other debris and hot lava would be cascading from the cliff above them.

They swam as far as they could and then treaded water, looking back towards the island now covered entirely in ash, smoke and steam plumes. It was as though the island had vanished before their eyes.

"Magdalene, everyone on the island must have been killed. No one could have survived," said Edmond. "A tsunami may form. It is best that we continue to swim seaward."

Edmond sensed that they had been saved from almost certain death at the clutches of the volcano and the O'Deas. "Perhaps everyone pursuing us has been killed," he said, spitting seawater out of his mouth.

He felt strongly that Elizabeth and her father had been tortured to find out their whereabouts, then murdered. A profound sadness came over him as he turned once more to look at the island.

In the distance a British destroyer could be seen looking for survivors. Edmond took his shirt off and waved it frantically at the ship. "Look! Look! They are turning towards us. God is merciful!"

They were helped aboard the destroyer and taken to the enlisted mess for questioning. "Are you both citizens of Montserrat?" asked the warrant officer.

Edmond replied, "That is correct."

"What are your names?"

"John O'Dea and my wife is Mary."

"Do you have any papers?"

"No, everything was destroyed on the island. We barely made it to sea. We lost not only our property but people we loved."

"I am sorry for your loss," the warrant officer said as though he was reading from a script.

"Since Montserrat is a protectorate of Britain, you automatically have British citizenship. We will transfer you to a container ship heading for England. There you will be given clothes and some money after you are processed ashore.

Chapter 6
COTE D'OR

They lay on the warm sands of Cote d'Or. The pebble-strewn beach was located not far from Cannes. The sun felt warm upon their skin. Magdalene turned on her side and faced the man that she had grown to love.

"Edmond, I still can't believe we are alive. Who would have ever predicted that you and I could become wealthy? We have beaten all of the odds. When you opened the satchel I expected to find nothing but black-and-white photographs and some old letters. Who would have thought that Ann, aided by Elizabeth, started all of this when they stole the Tears of Christ from the house of Mr. O'Dea. No wonder he was willing to do anything to get it back."

Magdalene continued, "I still find it hard to believe what the cross is made of. Christ made of pure Incan gold. Of course, the most striking item was the blue diamond above the crown of thorns. Did you look at the size of the emeralds that were mounted on the arms of the cross? And the artistic use of rubies to form the blood that ran from his side, the hands and feet? The buyer said that the Tears of Christ was priceless considering its history. No wonder he was so anxious to purchase it from us regardless of the cost. I am certain the world will never have an opportunity to see it again. That thought saddens me."

She turned on her back, shielding the hot rays of the sun with her hand. "Edmond, do you have your iPad with you? I would like to check the weather along the Riviera in case we want to go on to Switzerland later in the week. The heat here is really oppressive. It might do us good to go somewhere cooler."

"Sure. It is in the satchel just above my head," replied Edmond as he continued to read a novel.

She reached behind Edmond and picked up the iPad just as it buzzed. "A new message on Facebook for you. Now who would be sending you a message? I thought you changed your name again to Max Fuller?"

"I did," he replied.

"Why are you still on Facebook when no one knows you now?"

"I wanted to see what is happening to some of my friends since I no longer exist. People are not so careful when choosing 'friends' on Facebook. Max Fuller has several hundred new friends already."

"Oh wait just a moment," said Magdalene as she looked at his Facebook page. "An Ann Pennington has added a photograph to your Timeline, but I do not see anything there."

Edmond looked at her and smiled.

About the Author

Franklin Lafayette King was born in the Panhandle of Texas and spent much of his youth on the Blackland Prairie. He received a commission through the University of Texas in Austin and soon became involved in the Vietnam Conflict. After additional academic preparation, he moved to the foothills of the Appalachians. In addition to combat, he experienced both the eyes of a hurricane and an F-4 tornado, events that were to influence much of his later work.

www.ingramcontent.com/pod-product-compliance
Lightning Source LLC
Chambersburg PA
CBHW020404030726
47496CB00007B/2290